Also by Carolyn Brown

Secrets
in the
Sand

CAROLYN
BROWN

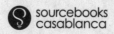

sourcebooks
casablanca

Published by Sourcebooks Casablanca, an imprint of Sourcebooks
P.O. Box 4410, Naperville, Illinois 60567-4410
(630) 961-3900
sourcebooks.com

Originally published as *Winning Angel* in 1998 in the United States by Kensington.

Printed and bound in Canada.
MBP 10 9 8 7 6 5 4 3 2 1

In memory of

my sister, Patti...who loved happy endings!

Dear Readers,

I'm so thankful for the opportunity to bring this story up-to-date. Written more than twenty years ago, it was among the very first four books I was fortunate enough to get published. A lot has happened since 1998. Attitudes have changed. Cell phones and computers have become the new normal.

It's been fun to look back and then look forward as I worked on Clancy and Angela's story. I have a lot of folks to thank for their help in doing this job. Thanks to my agency, Folio Management, and to my agent, Erin Niumata, for everything they do. Thanks to Deb Werksman for working with me on this new edition, and to all my readers for their support and love through the past twenty-two years and through more than a hundred books. And thanks to my husband, Mr. B, who is my biggest supporter! All of you deserve a standing ovation.

As I finished rewriting the story—with Clancy and Angela sitting on my desk and telling me how they felt—it was like leaving old friends behind. I hope you feel the same way when you read the last chapter.

Until next time,
Carolyn Brown

Chapter 1

CLANCY MORGAN DIDN'T PLAN TO GO TO THE TISHOMINGO Alumni Reunion but changed his mind at the last minute. The banquet part of the evening was almost over when he arrived, so he stood in the back and scanned the room from the shadows. Evidently, one of his classmates from ten years before had done the same thing, because a woman stood over behind a huge fake tree just inside the double doors leading into the ballroom. Clancy's dark brows drew down until they were almost a solid line above his chocolate-brown eyes. Something about her silhouette looked familiar, but it had been a while since he'd seen most of his former classmates, and he couldn't make out her face in the dim lighting. Perhaps she hadn't been a member of his graduating class, but was someone's wife, or else their plus one.

A vision popped into his mind of a girl who used to stand like that with one hand on her hip. He shook the memory out of his mind. Angela wouldn't show up to a noisy ten-year high school class reunion, not as shy as she had been.

"And now, please welcome Martha Simpson, the valedictorian of the class of 1953, and the woman who keeps this alumni association going," intoned the master of ceremonies from the podium. "Isn't she wonderful?"

The crowd applauded as a frail, elderly woman made her way to the front. Clancy sneaked in and sat down at the first table with an available empty chair.

"Martha Simpson is probably the only living member of that class," Laura Sides Walls whispered to him.

Clancy smiled and applauded dutifully with the rest of the alumni. When he looked back to see if the mystery woman was still standing in the shadows, she was gone. Nothing was there but the doors swinging to and fro, as if she had seen enough and left. Clancy wished he had gone over just in case she had been Angela.

"Damn," he mumbled under his breath. "Now she's gone, and I'll probably never see her again."

Martha leaned in close to the microphone and held up her palm for them to stop the applause. "Thank you all, but really, I'm just good at delegating, and I managed to live to be eighty-five. I always told that Emily Jacobs that I'd be famous someday."

Everyone laughed and clapped even harder.

"Welcome to the Tishomingo Alumni Banquet and Reunion," Martha went on, "a place where we're all seventeen or eighteen. Ever realize that when we come to these affairs, we're all seniors in high school again? Too damn bad that we don't look like we did then."

Clancy laughed with everyone else, but he couldn't get Angela Conrad off his mind.

━━━━━

Angel was aware that he had spotted her. She had felt the questions in his soft brown eyes, but she wasn't ready to face him. Before the evening was over, he would know who she was if she had to sit in his lap and tell him herself. But for now, she had to get ready. The sound equipment was in place, the microphones set up, the amps ready to bring the house down, and the rest of her band members were in the bus.

Angel slung open the door, stomped up the steps, and slumped down on the short sofa on the far wall. She crossed her arms over her chest, sucked in a lungful of air, and let it out slowly.

"Did you see Clancy?" Bonnie asked.

All of the members of the band were blonds except Angela. Patty and Susan were the same height, but Bonnie stood at just under six feet tall when she wore her cowboy boots.

"Yes," Angel answered. "Looking just as egotistical and full of himself as ever. And he's even sexier than he was ten years ago."

"Methinks I hear a note of love gone wrong. Hey, sounds like a good title for our new song. Maybe I just got the inspiration for the *Billboard* chart–topping song that we've needed all these years to take us straight to the top in Nashville." Patty pulled on her boots and twisted her straw-colored hair up in a twist.

Susan tossed Angel's cowboy hat across the bus. With her honey-blond hair and round face, some folks said that she could have been Miranda Lambert's sister. "Right. Just when we've decided to give up touring."

Angel caught her hat and laid it beside her. She stuck out her tongue at her friends, stood up and peeled faded jean shorts down over her hips and tossed them beside the hat. She jerked her knit tank top over her head, threw it in the direction of her shorts, and slipped on a black silk kimono-style robe.

"Hey, girls, I want to thank you again for tonight. Only real friends would play a two-bit gig like this, and I appreciate it. Means a lot to me." She sat down in front of a built-in vanity, complete with mirror and track lighting, and slapped makeup on her face, covering a fine sprinkling of freckles across her upturned nose. She outlined her big green eyes with a delicate tracing of dark pencil, then brushed mascara on her thick lashes. She flipped her dark-brown hair around her face with a styling comb and sat back to look at her reflection. Not bad for a backward girl who'd been scared of her own shadow ten years ago.

She wondered if anyone would recognize her. Not that Angel had planned to attend this reunion any more than the other nine that had already gone by. But then she had received the letter from the class president and decided—without exactly knowing why—that she'd come to this one. Some of the alumni might doubt she'd even been in their class when they saw her onstage, but after tonight, they'd go home and drag out their yearbooks to find her name and picture. And there she would be in big glasses, which she'd since replaced with contacts, and wildly curly hair, which she still couldn't tame.

Tonight, Angel was going to put away the past and forget about the pain. The self-help books she'd read and her therapist both told her to face her fear. Tonight she was doing just that. Tomorrow she was going to wake up a brand-new woman, ready to face whatever life might bring her, and she was never going to think about Clancy again.

She forced a smile at her reflection and then reached up and peeled the letter from the class president off her mirror. The committee had asked for a brief paragraph listing her accomplishments in the decade since she'd finished high school. Her short biography would be published in the alumni newsletter that would be sent out the next week. They had also asked for a contribution of some kind to the reunion. Angel had written back and offered to bring her band and play for the dance—free of charge.

"Better jerk them jeans on, darlin'." Mindy came out of the small bathroom and looked at Angel in the mirror. "Clancy Morgan's eyes would pop out of his head if you got to gyratin' your hips in nothing but that cute little lacy bra and underpants. I can't wait to see his face. Be sure you do something so that we know which one of the guys is the man who broke your heart."

"Oh, hush." Angel giggled as she stood up and took her

freshly starched white jeans from a hanger and shimmied into them. Then she topped them with a sequined vest with flashing red and white horizontal stripes on the right side and white stars on a ground of blue on the left.

"Lord, all I need is a couple of pasties with tassels." Angel checked her appearance in the mirror one last time.

"Hey, we're playing a gig for a bunch of high school alumni. We ain't doing a show for Neddie's Nudie Beauties. Time to go, ladies. Ten minutes until showtime." Allie, the shortest one in the band and the one with the lightest blond hair, crossed the floor and pushed open the bus door to lead the way.

"Y'all look wonderful." Angel was proud of her five friends in her band. They wore identical black jeans and black denim vests with the state flag of Texas embroidered on the backs.

"We clean up pretty good," Susan agreed. "You'd never know we were plain old working women the rest of the week."

The band members laughed and headed for the ballroom.

———

"Let's give the equipment one more check before they open the doors between the banquet room and this ballroom," Allie said. "Testing." She blew into the first microphone, which produced an ear squeal, and she nodded toward Bonnie, who was adjusting the amplifiers.

"Smoke machine is...ready," Mindy said from the side of the stage.

Allie turned a knob or two, double-checked the timer, then sat down at her drums and gave a warm-up roll with the sticks. "Ready to rock and roll," she growled into the microphone beside her.

"Ready," Susan breathed into her microphone, and drew her bow across her fiddle, creating a haunting sound that made Angel's blood curdle, just as it did every time they played.

"Then let's knock 'em dead." Mindy stretched her fingers and warmed up on the keyboard with a few bars of Miranda Lambert's "Hush, Hush."

The double doors from the banquet room swung open into the ballroom, and people wandered in, not quite sure this was where they belonged. Clancy Morgan and several companions found a table right in front of the small knockdown stage Angel toted around in the equipment trailer behind the bus. Even its slight elevation of twelve inches gave the band an advantage, which was better than being stuck back in a corner of a room on the same level as all the dancers.

"Dark in here," Angel heard a man say. "These itty-bitty candles on the tables don't give much light."

"You didn't complain about that ten years ago at the prom." His wife giggled. "Matter of fact, you wanted to blow the candles out so the ballroom would be darker."

"Yeah, but back then you were fun to be with in the dark," he teased.

The woman pouted.

Angel thought she recognized him—wasn't he Jim Moore?

The alarm on Allie's watch went off, and she did a roll on the drums and pushed a hidden button with her foot. The smoke machine emitted trails of white fog across the stage, and a rotating strobe picked up every flicker of candlelight from the tables. When the smoke began to clear, there were five Texas state flags facing the darkened room. Then, from somewhere behind a huge amplifier, Angel stepped out, all aglitter in red, white, and blue sequins.

"Good evening, ladies and gentlemen," she said in a deep, throaty voice. "I'm Angel—and this is the Honky Tonk Band. There's Allie on the drums." She stepped aside, and Allie stood up, bowed, and gave the audience fifteen seconds of a percussion riff.

"And Patty on rhythm guitar." One of the flags turned

around to reveal a honey-blond woman, who struck a chord and waved to the people.

Angel hoped for an enthusiastic crowd. Lord, but she hated to play to a dead bunch, and these alumni sure didn't look as lively as the folks they'd played to last night.

"Bonnie on steel," she said and the second flag turned.

Bonnie made the guitar slung around her neck whine like a baby.

"Susan on the fiddle." Angel waved to her left, and a short woman with platinum-colored hair perched a fiddle on her shoulder and let them hear a tantalizing bit of a classic country tune.

"And over here is Mindy on the keyboard." Mindy did a few chords of Floyd Cramer's "Last Date."

Then the final flag turned slowly to face the alumni of Tishomingo High School. "Hi, y'all," Angel said huskily into the mic.

"And this is Angel!" Martha stepped up to the microphone. "You might remember her as Angela Conrad. She and these gorgeous band members have agreed to play for us tonight for free. Let's make them welcome and get ready for a show. These ladies will be at the Twisted Spur Honky Tonk in Davis next Friday night for their final gig, so we're lucky to get 'em. Angel says she's tired of working all week and the weekends too. So, give them a big hand to let them know how much we appreciate them playing for us." She started the applause and the audience followed suit as she left the stage and grabbed a young guy's hand, led him to the dance floor and nodded to Angel to start the party.

"Wind 'em up, girls," Angel whispered. She grabbed a mic and started the evening with a surefire crowd-pleaser. Mindy tinkled the keyboard keys and Allie kept a steady beat with the brushes on the drums. Angel strutted across the stage, sequins flashing in the strobe lights, and the long diamond drops that dangled from her ears glittering in her dark-brown shoulder-length curls.

Before long, there were at least twenty couples in the middle of the floor, dancing in one way or another. Several were doing something between the twist and the jerk, and an older couple was executing a pretty fine jitterbug. Angel kept looking down at the table where Clancy Morgan sat alone while his friends tried to keep up with the beat on the dance floor. Evidently, Melissa—if he had married her—couldn't accompany him tonight. Or maybe he hadn't married her. Now wouldn't that be a hoot?

Angel put her left hand on her hip and struck a pose, and memories from that summer ten years ago flooded Clancy's mind, again. What had happened to the Angela Conrad he'd known? She was supposed to marry old Billy Joe Summers and raise a shack full of snotty-nosed kids. She was supposed to work in a sewing factory, supporting Billy Joe's life-threatening drinking habit. She wasn't supposed to be on a stage, belting out songs by famous artists.

Patty started a strong rhythm and Angel stepped off the stage and mixed with the people in the dancing crowd, singing into a cordless mic. Then she sat down on the table right in front of Clancy, wiggled her shoulders, and sang to him as she looked right in his eyes. He wanted to say something, but what could he say? Words wouldn't turn him from a jerk into a decent guy, so he just sat there without saying a word, shaking his head in disbelief.

She looked something like the old Angela, except she wasn't wearing glasses. She leaned toward him far enough that he could see down the front of her vest, and a red heat stirred inside him as he remembered her body against his. She kept singing while the girls provided backup on the stage. Then suddenly, before he could blink, she was back on the stage.

"Hey, Mike Griffin, pull that woman up a little closer. You sure danced closer than that when we were in high school," Angel teased in the middle of another song, a more romantic one, while the band played the break.

She glanced at the table to her left and saw that Clancy still had a bewildered look on his face, as if his eyes couldn't believe his ears. Angel could still list his every accomplishment. Quarterback from tenth through twelfth grade, taking the team to the state championship all three years. Debate champion, too, winning the regional trophy during his senior year.

Angel would bet dollars to doughnuts that if Clancy had to hop up on the stage right now and speak, he'd be as awkward as he'd been that summer night just before everyone was leaving for college. He couldn't hide his feelings then, and he obviously still hadn't learned how. Because his long face told her he was having a hard time dealing with her putting on a show for the alumni organization. In fact, his ego appeared to be *severely* deflated.

"We'll have a fifteen-minute break while we grab something to drink." Allie pulled her microphone close to her face. "See y'all in a quarter of an hour."

Before Clancy could make sense of his thoughts, Angel had gone out the side door, surrounded by her band. He stretched out his long limbs, amazed that he'd sat still for an hour and a half while memories and her presence tormented him. He smiled and nodded at several of his old friends as he made his way to the doors leading out to the balcony, from which he could see the bus parked in the lot behind the ballroom. It was black with gold metallic lettering that sparkled in the light from the streetlamps. The word *Angel* had a crooked halo slung over the capital *A*, and *The Honky Tonk Band* had little gold devils with pitchforks sitting on each *o*.

He remembered the nights when she'd sung along with the radio in his new red Camaro, and he hadn't been able to tell which was the real singer and which was Angela. Who would have ever thought she'd be running around in her own bus with a band of women who looked like candidates for the Dallas Cowboy Cheerleaders?

Tonight had been crazy. Clancy hadn't even thought about Angela showing up. She was almost the one voted most likely *not* to succeed. Although hardly a day had gone by in the past ten years that something didn't make him think of Angela Conrad, he'd long since learned to disassociate himself from what had really happened that summer. It was as if it happened to someone in a book, and he'd just read about it. He hadn't really sat on the creek bank with her late into the nights and let the minnows nibble their toes. He hadn't actually walked away that last night, knowing she was crying. No, it couldn't have been him. It was someone else in a novel or a movie, and he just remembered the details too well.

———

"Whew." Allie dabbed her face with a tissue. "Pretty lively crowd for a bunch of has-beens."

"Hey." Angel giggled nervously. "I graduated from this place. I belong to that crowd."

"Yeah, like I belong at the pearly gates of heaven." Susan's blue eyes twinkled. "You outgrew them years ago. Don't let these hicks make you think you still belong to their world."

"Thanks." Angel pretended to slap her cheek. "I needed that."

"Well, I can see why you were so stuck on that Clancy. He fills out them Wranglers pretty damned good." Patty sighed. "And those big, wide shoulders about gave me the vapors." She fluttered her long eyelashes. "Maybe you oughta give him another chance, Angel. Lord, handsome as he is, I'd give him a chance if he wasn't already wearin' your brand."

"Hell," Angel snorted. "He never wore my brand. He's free for the taking if you're interested. I don't think he's still married. If he is, his wife didn't come with him. But rest assured he's about as trustworthy as those two little devils painted on the side of this bus."

"No, thanks," Patty said, putting on fresh lipstick. "You can keep him. Then tame him or kill him, but don't give him to me."

"Me neither." Mindy gulped in the hot night air and looked up at the starlit sky to see if there might be a stray cloud with a few raindrops to spare. "Hey, look up on the balcony when you come outside, Angel. Clancy's up there staring down here like he can't believe his little eyeballs."

"Yeah? That's nothing new. He always did look down on me." Angel was suddenly tired. Her bones ached as never before during a performance…and so did her stupid heart. "Another hour and a half and we'll take this bus home and park it. Then I'll forget about Clancy Morgan and get on with life. I was here for closure, and I've got it."

"Sure, you do." Bonnie chuckled. "You'll forget Clancy

when you're stone-cold dead and planted six feet down. Women don't forget first loves, and they *never* forget a first love who did them dirty."

Chapter 2

ANGEL FLIPPED THE LIGHT SWITCH JUST INSIDE THE MASSIVE doors of her office and slipped off her shoes. She padded across the thick ivory carpet and plopped down in an oversize blue velvet chair behind an antique French provincial desk. She tossed the alumni newsletter on the desk, laced her hands behind her head, and tried to calm down.

She'd gone to the reunion to give her former classmates a dose of comeuppance. She had planned to leave with a smile on her face and never think about any of them again. Several former acquaintances had made a point of stopping by the stage between songs and saying hello to her, but Clancy left just after the last song without a word. But then, what could he say? He'd made his choice ten years ago, and there was no room for a change of heart.

Angel got up and went to the window. Patty was the last one leaving the parking lot. The other girls had already left in the early-morning darkness. Next Friday they would be playing at a honky-tonk just south of Davis, Oklahoma, and then a new band called The Gamblers would pick up the bus and have it repainted with their logo. It was high time for the Honky Tonk Band to go out with a flourish and retire. The girls enjoyed performing, but they needed their weekends these days. Allie was married and her husband, Tyler, complained that he never saw her on weekends. Susan lived with her boyfriend, Richie, and they needed more quality time together.

Bonnie was engaged and planning an October wedding, and Mindy was in the middle of a divorce. Besides, none of them were getting any younger. Angel sighed, thinking about how she could catch up on all the work at the farm when she stopped touring, and she had this oil business to run as well.

She thought about Tishomingo again. Main Street had changed a little in the past ten years. The courthouse was new, and the café where she and her grandmother had an occasional burger had a different name these days, and there was a new chiropractor's office on the corner of Main and Broadway. Blake Shelton's businesses were where a clothing store and a drugstore used to stand. She'd looked upstream at Pennington Creek when they'd crossed the bridge over it into town and noticed that it hadn't changed at all. The same trees still shaded the sandbar below the dam, and the memories of what had happened night after night on a blanket in the privacy of those trees were so real, she could almost smell Clancy's aftershave.

Angel picked up the newsletter and began to read. Each page had a classmate's name at the top and a summary of their accomplishments in the past ten years. Apparently, almost everyone had sent in the questionnaire no matter whether they could attend the alumni banquet and the dance. She found her own bio and reread it. *I'm not enclosing a bio, but my band and I—Angel and the Honky Tonk Band—will play for the dance free of charge if you would like. Let me know at the following address. Angela Conrad.* She'd added a box number in Denison, Texas. But no one knew that she had rented the box for one month just for the return answer to her letter.

She scanned down the letter to what Clancy had written. Since leaving high school, he'd graduated from the University of Oklahoma with a bachelor's degree in geology and chemistry and a minor in education. Then he'd enlisted in the air force and had been stationed in Virginia for most of his four-year career and had gone to graduate school for a master's in education. Just recently he'd come back to Oklahoma and started teaching in an Oklahoma City high school. Under *Marital Status*, he had marked an X beside *Divorced*.

So, he probably had married Melissa after all. But what had happened? By small-town society's rules, Mr. and Mrs. Clancy Morgan were supposed to be living happily ever after. Suddenly, Angel wished she had subscribed to the Tishomingo weekly newspaper. Then at least she would have known who'd married whom, who had children, and so forth.

When her granny had driven their old green pickup truck out of Tishomingo that long-ago fall day, Angel hadn't even looked back in the rearview mirror for one last glimpse of the place where she'd lived since she was three years old. She hadn't left anything behind but heartaches, and she didn't need to look back at the fading lights of town to recapture them. They would be with her forever.

She looked through the newsletter to see what Billy Joe Summers was doing these days. She hadn't seen him at the dance even though she'd scanned the ballroom several times to see if there was a six-foot, five-inch gangly man standing shyly on the sidelines. Billy Joe had always been nice to her, and that awful night on the sandbar when she'd sat with her feet in the warm water, it had been Billy Joe's name that Clancy had mentioned so scornfully.

"Hello again, Mr. Henry." Angel picked up a worn teddy bear sitting on top of her filing cabinet and held him, just for old times' sakes. Mr. Henry had listened sympathetically to all her tales of woe in the years since she'd been given him for her fifth birthday...and here she was, still feeling sorry for herself.

She wondered how her memories of Tishomingo could still be so vivid. After all, she hadn't ever wanted to go back, even though she and her granny had lived there for fifteen years, since the day she'd turned three years old. Angel had spent her babyhood in nearby Kemp, and although they visited her great-grandpa at the farm there a couple of times a year, she couldn't recollect anything about it.

When Angel had turned eighteen, her great-grandpa Poppa John had died and left his twenty acres to his only child—Angel's grandmother. After his estate had been settled, Angel and her granny had left Tishomingo and gone back to Kemp. And it hadn't happened a minute too soon, in anyone's opinion. Memories flooded her mind. "Don't stay out late, Angela. We've got to pack in the morning," her granny had reminded her. "Got to be out of the house before midnight or pay more rent, you know."

"I know." Angela had gone out the front door and walked west toward the dam. All summer she'd gone swimming every evening in Pennington Creek, and it was a good thing August had arrived, because her bikini was beginning to look as worn-out as her jeans. Most times, it seemed like just a hop, skip, and jump from her house to the swimming hole, but that evening the walk took forever.

Angel had shimmied out of her shorts and shirt, tugged the top of her bikini down and the bottoms up before she sat down on the sandbar and waited for Clancy. She picked up a twig and drew an interlocking heart in the sand. She put her initial in one heart, Clancy's in the second one, and wrote *baby* in the part that interlocked. She loved him, and he loved her. The secret that they had been hiding all summer would come out as soon as she told him her news. Sure, they were young, but she had a scholarship, and he didn't have to go to Oklahoma University. The important thing was that they would be together.

She soaked her feet in the lukewarm water while she waited. Clancy wouldn't be there for another half hour so she thought about all the scenarios lying ahead. She'd known the first time they'd accidentally met each other in this very place that she was flirting with big trouble, but she'd been in love with Clancy Morgan since kindergarten. If he would just touch her hand or kiss her one time before she moved away, she could survive forever on the memories. That he didn't want anyone to know they were dating stung a little, but now their secret would be out in public. Clancy was a good guy. He would do the right thing.

She was so deep in her thoughts that she didn't even hear the car tires crunching on gravel when he drove up close to the sandbar. He sat down beside her, and she quickly ran a hand over the heart she had drawn. He was a smart guy. If he saw the secret in the sand, he would know immediately why she was smiling so big. She wanted to tell him and then feel his arms around her, and hear him telling her that everything would be fine.

Clancy plopped down on the sandbar. Usually he drew her into his arms and kissed her the minute he arrived, but not that night. "We need to talk, Angela."

"Yes, we do," she said as she scooted over closer to him and wrapped her arms around his neck. "I'll go first. I'm pregnant."

Her heart broke when he pushed her away. It shattered

into a million pieces when he said, "I can't marry you or even live with you. Billy Joe has been in love with you since first grade. He won't care if the baby isn't really his."

"Go to hell, Clancy," she'd found enough courage to say. "I don't need you anyway. I can take care of myself. They don't stone women for being single mamas, so just go."

There had been a lot more to the fight, but she couldn't bear to remember any more of the details. She wiped away a tear as that last visual of Clancy popped into her mind.

With a shrug and a relieved expression, he had turned and jogged up the bank to his car. She watched the trail of dust follow him all the way to where he turned left to cross the bridge, and when the Camaro was out of sight, Angela had buried her face in her hands and sobbed, heartbroken and alone.

Angel pulled her thoughts back to the present and wiped away the tears. She returned to the newsletter page and flipped through until she found Billy Joe's bio. He was living in San Francisco, where he was working as a computer technician. Under *Comments* he had written: *I want to tell Angela Conrad hello wherever she is. I'm married to Stephen and we have an adopted son, Adam. We are both very active in the gay rights movement and have had articles published in several papers and magazines.*

Her amused response started as a weak giggle, grew into a chuckle, and then a full-fledged roar. So Billy Joe had finally come out with the news. She hoped Clancy Morgan had read Billy Joe's contribution to the alumni newsletter. Perhaps it would help him remember his asinine remark to her that long-ago night beside Pennington Creek.

———

Clancy let himself into the house where he had grown up. His father had died while he was in Virginia with the air force, and now his mother, Meredith, lived there alone. She was already sleeping, so he tiptoed to the dining room where he turned on the light above the table and set his newsletter down.

He put on a pot of coffee, and when it finished dripping, he poured himself a mug, sat down at the table, and turned to Angela Conrad's brief bio. His heart fluttered softly, then dropped to a dull ache when he read what she'd written. He still didn't know anything, except that she probably lived in Denison, since she gave a box number there. She'd given no personal information and Clancy wondered if she was married, single, or divorced. She didn't mention if she had a child or children, and she was still using her maiden name.

Clancy burned his lip on the hot coffee and swore softly. "Damn it all," he muttered, but he was angry with more than the coffee. He was mad at himself all over again as he remembered that hot August night when he'd gone to see her to break it off. Angela had been waiting for him in her usual place, with her feet in the water, wearing the same bikini that she'd worn all summer. Her jean shorts and that orange T-shirt that was too big for her were tossed up on the creek bank. Her brown curls were pulled back into a ponytail, and she looked like a little girl. But then she was only five foot three and barely weighed 110 pounds.

He remembered telling her to marry Billy Joe Summers and her telling him to go to hell. And he'd never seen her again, from that night until now.

That night he'd gone to the Dairy Queen. Melissa was there and had flirted with him. They both wound up at Oklahoma University and started dating during the first semester. At the end of the first semester, he had casually asked a former classmate about Billy Joe and Angela and learned that both had left Tishomingo at about the same time, and that was all anyone knew.

He and Melissa had married right after their college graduation, and she'd taught school while he was in the air force.

He'd thought they were doing fine until the year she'd come home and told Clancy she wanted out. She'd fallen in love with the principal of her school, and they were planning to marry as soon as the divorce was final. That had ended what he'd thought would be a military career. Clancy had come back to Oklahoma, gotten his master's degree, and landed his present job teaching chemistry at an Oklahoma City high school.

He turned the pages until he found Billy Joe Summers's name. Maybe Billy Joe lived in Denison too…and maybe he'd married Angela after all, and they had had that pack of kids and she and her band played border-town dives just to pay the bills.

But when Clancy read Billy Joe's page, he felt just plain foolish. Billy Joe was gay, and Angela sure hadn't looked poor. Two-bit bands that played for border-town dives didn't have customized buses, and none of them had smoke machines and their own knockdown stages, and none of them played at alumni reunions either. Angela and her band had done well. Evidently, they hadn't hit the big time, but she and Billy Joe had both done well. And now her name was Angel.

He'd called her that sometimes, he realized.

So just what in the hell was she up to? *None of your damn*

business, his conscience told him. *You gave up any rights to know what she was doing with her life that August night down by the creek when you were eighteen years old.*

He turned out the light and went to the living room where he leaned back in his father's recliner and thought about Angela Conrad. His angel—once upon a time.

———————

Angel turned off her office lights and pulled the door shut. She carried a burgundy leather briefcase in one hand and her laptop in the other. She pushed the button for the elevator to take her down to the ground-floor garage where her black Jaguar was parked. It was time to go home. The two-story Conrad Oil Enterprises, Inc. building disappeared in her rear-view mirror as she drove to Main Street in Denison and then east on a farm road.

She thought about the first days when she and the girls had formed the band and played the border-town dives in Cartwright, Colbert, Yuba, and Willis. They didn't even have a name then, just a few instruments and a need to make a couple of dollars on the weekends to keep them in college. That was before Conrad Oil Enterprises had been even a glimmer of an idea.

One night they'd unloaded their equipment at the Dixie Pixie club in Yuba while an old man wearing faded overalls watched. He swilled his liquor from a mason jar and said to his wife, a big woman in red stretch pants, "Well, looky here, Momma. There's a pretty little angel with her honky-tonk band. Guess we died and went to heaven." The old man had named their band right then, and Angel wondered if he was even around anymore to know how far she and the Honky Tonk Band had come in the past years.

She crossed the river bridge and turned left into Hendrix, Oklahoma, then drove several more miles to her farm. It was only twenty acres, but it was home, and home was where her heart was this morning.

The sun was an orange ball on the horizon when she pulled the car into the oval driveway. When she opened the door, she could smell the welcoming fragrance of roses. Jimmy's gardening skills kept the rosebushes looking wonderful, even if the Oklahoma winds and hot, blistering sun tried to rob the blooms at this time of year. But, as she'd told him so many times, his thumbs were greener than spring grass, and he could make silk plants reproduce if he wanted to. The house was dark, but then she hadn't expected her housekeeper, Hilda, to be there yet. She didn't usually arrive until midmorning and then left in the middle of the afternoon, unless Angel was there and needed her longer.

She opened the gate to the white picket fence surrounding the two-story farmhouse that looked like it had been there since the turn of the century. But she'd had the house custom-built just four years before. It was her dream house, and Angel loved everything about it. She crossed the veranda that wrapped the house on three sides and noticed that the blue morning glories climbing the porch posts were starting to open with the approach of dawn. She unlocked the front door. Arriving early in the morning and grabbing a few hours by herself after a gig was just what she needed that morning. She'd wanted closure, but she sure hadn't gotten any. If anything, she was more agitated than ever.

She boiled a kettle of water and poured it over green tea leaves in a ceramic pot and waited for the tea to steep. She propped up her feet on the hassock beside the cold fireplace and watched the sun come up through the French doors leading out onto the patio. As the sun topped the well house, she could see the silhouette of her first oil well, now standing as a silent sentinel to all that was hers, and the beginning of the successful enterprise known as Conrad Oil, which had grown so fast it still didn't seem quite real.

Dawn was gone and a new Sunday was born before Angel poured the lukewarm tea in a cup and put a slice of Hilda's homemade bread in the toaster. Granny would have liked this house. She would have fussed about the cost of it, but she would have grinned that big smile that made her eyes disappear in a face so full of wrinkles it looked like a road map. And she would have turned over in her grave if she knew Angel paid a gardener these days to keep the roses blooming and the morning glories watered, and had a housekeeper. But then, when Granny had inherited this property from her father and moved with Angel to the original three-room house on these twenty acres, Angel hadn't owned an oil company.

Angel buttered the bread with sweet butter. Someday she might have to watch fat grams and calories, but not today. She liked real butter on her toast, just as her granny had. Thoughts of the past flitted through her mind.

She and her grandmother had arrived with all their belongings in the back of that old, rusty green truck that looked like an accident waiting for a place to happen. The old house had only three rooms—a small living room and kitchen, a tiny bathroom, and one bedroom where she and Granny put their twin beds. They'd lived there happily enough until four years later, when her granny had died peacefully in her sleep.

The preacher had read a poem and the Twenty-Third Psalm at the graveside service, and a few church members showed up along with the girls in her band. Three months later, Angel had mortgaged the property and drilled a gusher. From there, she'd taken one giant step after another, until today she was the major stockholder and president of her own oil company, based in Denison, with branch offices in Oklahoma and Louisiana.

Angel closed her eyes. She had all the money she could spend in a lifetime…all the excitement of unexpected success…all the peacefulness of a country home to enjoy for the rest of her life…but none of it would ever ease the cold, blue loneliness in her heart.

Chapter 3

THE NEXT FRIDAY NIGHT, CLANCY PARKED HIS FORD BRONCO a comfortable distance away from the big, black bus sitting in the crowded parking lot of the Twisted Spur Honky Tonk, just off I-35 south of Davis. He could hear the *thump, thump, thump* of the music every time the doors opened and someone went in or came back out.

He wanted to pay the cover charge and go inside to listen to Angel sing, to watch her move with that sexy confidence she hadn't had in high school, to breathe in the essence of her that sent his senses reeling, but he didn't want her to know he was there. He had thought at first that he would simply wait beside the bus and try to talk to her when she finished the gig.

Whether she liked it or not, he was going to find out what really happened after he went away to college. It occurred to him that he didn't deserve to know after the way he'd treated her, but perhaps she'd forgiven him. They were adults, now, after all, and he had a feeling that he wouldn't be at peace until he knew the whole story.

The doors opened, but it wasn't the band members who came out. A big man dressed in black jeans and cowboy boots with silver tips on the pointed toes stumbled out with his arm around a skinny, hard-looking blond wearing a denim mini-skirt and red cowboy boots. Then another couple staggered forth, giggling as they held each other up long enough to get the car door open and drive away. Angel finally came out of the honky-tonk with her band members and started loading equipment. The lady she'd introduced as Patty, the rhythm guitar player, sat down in the driver's seat and revved up the motor.

The bus pulled into the parking lot of an all-night convenience store across the highway from the honky-tonk. Patty went inside and came out carrying a big bag of chips and a brown bag full of what Clancy supposed was junk food. As he followed the bus, she made a sharp turn at the overpass bridge and headed south on the interstate.

Traffic was sparse at that time of night, so Clancy lingered a quarter of a mile behind them. They crossed the Red

River into Texas. The bus made a quick stop in Whitesboro, and one of the girls got out. Allie, the drummer, waved and hopped into a new-model red minivan and drove north. Then the bus went on to Denison.

Clancy managed to keep the taillights in view as the bus stopped and started through town, finally going down an alley and disappearing through huge garage doors in the bottom floor of an enormous building. He eased into a parking place reserved for banking customers only in the lot across the alley and studied the sign, which was lit up with overhead bulbs.

"Conrad Oil Enterprises?" he said aloud. "Holy cow. Angel must have a rich uncle." He wondered why she had never mentioned anyone in her family having money.

The garage doors opened again and four vehicles drove out of the building's garage. The first one was a dark Lincoln with the window rolled down, driven by Bonnie, the steel guitar player. A red Cadillac followed her, and Susan, the girl who'd played the fiddle, waved to the car behind her as she pulled out onto the road and went south. The third car was a black convertible with Mindy behind the wheel. The last one was a white pickup, and although Clancy could tell there was only one person in the truck, he didn't know if it was Patty or Angel. Just as he turned the key to start up the engine, he caught a glimpse of Angel, still wearing her sequined vest, standing beside the bus and watching the doors of the garage close.

Clancy slid down in the seat and waited an hour. Finally, just after dawn, a black Jaguar rolled out of the garage and turned north. He followed it out of the alley, down the side street, and onto Main Street where she turned right and almost lost him. Angel drove faster than the speed limit and crossed the railroad tracks as if they weren't even there. When he hit the tracks, he bounced around like a puppet inside a rain barrel, but he managed to hold on to the wheel and keep the back end of her car in sight. The road they were traveling had to have more doglegs in it than the city pound, twisting this way and that, and Angel never seemed to even tap the brakes.

Then her car made an abrupt left turn. He was sure that she glanced up in the rearview mirror and spotted him, but evidently, she hadn't, because she squealed the tires and took off across a bridge. The sides were so short that he could see the Red River down below, looking like a small creek rather than a river. Clancy hated heights. He didn't mind bridges that had something over the top or even tall sides, but this one looked like he could practically drive right over the edge of that short side. When he peered over the edge as he drove across, his heart did a flip-flop. Anything higher than a two-foot stepladder made him nervous. He shuddered again but didn't look down at the muddy water. Why in the devil would Angel want to take this route to her house when there had to be a perfectly good road somewhere else? Maybe she remembered he was afraid of heights and was torturing him.

The Jaguar took another sharp turn and sped down the road past a café on one side and a beer hall on the other. Then suddenly it stopped in front of him so fast that he almost slammed into the rear bumper. Before he could collect his wits, Angel had the door jerked open and was standing with her left hand on her hip, an angry look in her eye and a pistol in her right hand pointed right at his nose.

"Why in the hell are you following me?" she demanded, then realized who was behind the wheel. "Clancy? What in the hell are *you* following me for?"

"Well, I...I just..." he stammered. "Put that damn gun down, Angela. I'm not here to hurt you."

She lowered the weapon. "Just why the hell are you here?"

"I just wanted to know where you lived. I asked around and no one knew," he said honestly.

"Oh, and why were you asking about me?"

"Got a problem here, Miss Conrad?" A middle-aged policeman opened the door of the café.

"Nope. I thought I did, but it turns out I know this man," she told him.

"Sure?" the policeman asked cautiously as he noticed the gun still in her hand.

"Yes, I'm sure," she said. "He's an old classmate of mine. I'm fine, Bruce. Thanks for checking on me."

"Okay. I know you have a permit for that gun. But be careful who you point it at. If he really is an old classmate, I don't know why you have it out of your purse," the officer warned. He got into his black-and-white patrol car and drove away.

"We need to talk," Clancy demanded.

"Oh, really?" Angel growled at him. "Well, darlin', I wanted to talk about our future ten years ago. But you only gave me some unsolicited advice about marrying Billy Joe. So, what gives you the right to expect answers now?" Her hands shook so badly, she nearly dropped her pearl-handled .22 pistol. She couldn't decide whether she wanted to kill him... or kiss him.

"Maybe I don't have any right to talk to you at all," Clancy said. "I'll leave you alone if that's what you want.

I just wanted to satisfy my curiosity, I guess. I waited in the parking lot at that honky-tonk up in Davis and followed you. Do you work for that oil company or something?"

"It's none of your damned business where I work or what I do, and that's called stalking. Go home to your small town, Clancy. I'm not a naive little girl anymore. And I'm sure as hell not impressed with you. You want to talk, just follow me." She slammed the door to his car and stomped back to her vehicle.

Clancy noticed a sign that said Muddy Creek Road when they turned right and suddenly his tires were crunching over gravel, but Angel didn't slow down much. Just when he thought it was as bad as it could get, the road turned into little more than a pathway with tall weeds on either side towering over his vehicle. He'd need a machete to chop his way out of this mess if he ran out of gas. Grass grew at least knee-high in the middle of the two ruts, and he wondered if she was leading him out into the middle of someone's farm pond to drown him.

Then she whipped the Jaguar into a cemetery. She parked and got out of her car, crossed over to a grave, and dropped down on her knees in the fenced enclosure at the far east side of the little cemetery. He got out of his vehicle and followed her.

"I didn't want to come to a cemetery. I want to talk about what happened after that night after I left you at the creek," he said. "Is this where your grandmother is buried?" He read the name on the center granite stone, DOROTHY JUNE CONRAD, then turned and read the one to her right, JOHN HERMAN CONRAD. Before he could look at the one to the left, Angel was standing in front of the tombstone, shielding it.

"You don't deserve this," she declared.

"What happened, Angel? Did you marry someone? Did you have our baby and give it away, or did you keep it? God, I thought you'd embarrass me and tell everyone in Tishomingo it was mine, but you didn't. Then you were gone, and I was so relieved...but now—"

"But now what?" She tried to will the tears to dry up, but they dripped down her cheeks.

"I want to know what happened. Angel, give me some answers. What happened to our child?"

She stepped to one side and sat down on the park bench beside the third tombstone. "There is your answer," she whispered.

And he read aloud, "Clancy Morgan Conrad."

"Our son was stillborn. Eight pounds, and so beautiful he would take your breath away, but he couldn't live—not any more than your love for me could live. Now you've got your answers, so go away, Clancy Morgan, and leave me alone," she said through clenched teeth.

Chapter 4

Clancy's gut clenched. Tears filled his eyes. No wonder she hated him. He should walk away but he couldn't force his eyes away from his son's name, birthday, and death date—which were the same.

"Did he live long?" he asked.

"He didn't even take a breath. He was stillborn." Tears dripped off her jaw. "I wanted him so badly, but I didn't get to keep him. God punished me for being ashamed that I was pregnant. I'm going home. You can stay here as long as you want."

"Can we please talk some more?" he pleaded. "I'll leave you alone if you'll just talk to me."

"You can follow me home," she said, "but then I don't want to see you again after we talk."

He hurried back to his vehicle and once again fell in behind her. Emotions ran through his heart like they were on a fast roller coaster. He had a son, but he didn't, and Angel had named the baby after him after the way he'd treated her. She drove a mile to the north, and then took a road to the right and drove down a beautiful macadam lane with trees and flowers growing on both sides.

Angel didn't stop to smell the roses or enjoy the morning glories as she stomped across the wooden porch to the front door of the farmhouse. She opened the door and was about to flip the light switch when she heard the scrunch of gravel as Clancy drove up.

She heard his car door slam and turned to see Clancy walking up the flower-edged sidewalk to the porch. Her first thought was to pull that little revolver out of her purse and shoot him before he reached her porch; her second was to meet him halfway and drag him up to her bedroom.

"This where you live?" he asked casually. Leave it to Clancy to act as if nothing important had ever happened between them.

"No, this is where my boyfriend and I live together," she retorted as hatefully as she could, and then wondered where that lie came from.

"Oh, really?" He was beside her. "What's his name?"

"Nosy, aren't you?" she said.

"You still haven't told me the story of your life," he said calmly.

Clancy sat down in the porch swing as if he owned the place.

"I'm too tired and emotional to talk right now. If you really want to talk to me, then you can wait right here on the porch until I settle down. I need a few hours rest. I played a gig half the night, and I plan to work here all weekend. Looks like you've been up all night, too, but that's your problem, Clancy. Good night or morning or whatever. We'll talk when I wake up if you still want to hear anything about me," Angel said, and closed the door.

She bypassed the kitchen and went straight upstairs, took a quick shower and crawled into the four-poster bed. So now he knew where she lived and where she worked. She pulled a pillow over her eyes and willed her tired mind and body to go to sleep. She awoke in the middle of the afternoon. She could hear a lawn mower in the backyard, so evidently Jimmy was working back there. The noise of the vacuum cleaner in the living room let her know Hilda was busy.

What would her granny have told her to do about a

problem like Clancy ten years after that horrible night? Every word he'd said still rang in her ears. "Angela, you mean to say you aren't on the pill? Hellfire and damnation, I never would've—" Clancy stopped and glared at her. "Well, it won't work. I'm not going to marry you. Lord, I'd be the laughingstock of the whole damn town of Tishomingo."

"Did I ask you to marry me?" She looked up at him. "Go on to the Dairy Queen where all you popular kids hang out. I wouldn't want you to miss out on being with Melissa and the rest of your friends. Forget all about us. About everything we did this summer. Go have a happy life," she had said in a voice just barely above a whisper, hoarse with emotion.

"Don't you tell anyone that I got you pregnant." Clancy's eyes had flashed anger and the deep cleft in his chin had quivered. He'd raked his hand through his dark-brown hair, and he hadn't known whether to walk away or sit down and talk some more.

"I'll tell whoever I want." Angela had turned her back on him.

"I've got five hundred dollars of my graduation money left. I'll give it to you for an abortion," he had offered.

"Just go away, Clancy. I don't know why I ever thought I

loved you, anyway. It's a cinch you never did love me." She stood up and grabbed her shorts.

"Sit down," Clancy had said in a desperate tone. "Listen to me. There's a solution. Bob got Janie pregnant last year and they told everyone they were going to the mall in Oklahoma City and to the movies, and then he was taking her to her girlfriend's house for the night. They got a motel room and stayed in it after the abortion. Nothing bad happened."

Angela buttoned her shorts and sat down beside him. She put her feet in the water and watched the tiny fish nibble on her polished red toenails. "I didn't do this on purpose," she declared.

"Don't worry about it." He sighed. "My checkbook is in the car." He nodded toward the Camaro his parents had given him for graduation. "I suppose you can get someone to take you."

"Forget it."

"What are you going to do?" he asked. "Maybe you could marry Billy Joe Summers. You know he's been in love with you since we were little kids," he said sarcastically.

"I'm going home," she said as she got to her feet again. "I haven't really been in love with you, Clancy. I was in love with the boy I thought you were. Don't worry about this baby. Don't let the thought of it ever cross your mind again. It's not yours… It's mine, and I'll take care of it. Just go on home."

"Oh hell, Angela, use your brain. You're smart even if you are—"

"What?" She had scowled at him. "Poor? Well, that didn't stop you from kissing me and making love with me all summer, did it? I've been a complete fool about you, Clancy. Someday you're going to look back and think about tonight, though. And I hope your heart hurts when you do. I hope it aches just like mine is aching right now. But between now and then, don't ever think about this baby we made again." Angela walked away from him without looking back.

"Don't worry, honey," Granny had told her that night when she'd gone home crying. "He's a rich kid and he's not about to do right by you. He'll marry some stuck-up girl when he's had his fun and gets ready to settle down. We'll take care of ourselves. We'll be movin' tomorrow just like we planned, and you're goin' to college this fall on that grant money you got. Things look tough tonight, but it'll work out, Angela. Stop your weepin' and learn your lessons."

"But I love him, Granny," she had sobbed.

"I hope you do," her grandmother snorted. "Be a terrible

thing if you didn't. But cryin' ain't goin' to make anything different. We'll manage and nobody will ever know."

Angel shook her head, clearing the memories, and threw back the covers. She crawled out of bed, threw the covers over the pillows, and picked out an old pair of jeans from the closet. She wiggled down into them and jerked a T-shirt over her head. She pulled her curls up into a ponytail, put on a pair of sneakers, and was ready.

"Got a guest," Hilda said when she reached the kitchen. The housekeeper smiled in an odd way, and Angel wondered what had happened while she'd been sleeping.

"Where?" Angel asked.

"Out there on the swing. Asleep. Lot of man to be curled up like that. I told him to get out of here when I come in to work, but he said you knew he was there, and he wasn't leavin' until you talked to him. So I just ignored him. He's been asleep about two hours. Just sat there swinging most of the mornin'. He's been out there for hours," Hilda said.

"Clancy is a determined man, all right." Angel smiled.

"Oh," Hilda said. "So that's Clancy Morgan out there, is it? You should kick him off that swing and tell him to go to hell. I wouldn't give that man the sweat from my brow if he was dyin' of thirst." Hilda fumed as she picked up her broom and started toward the fireplace to sweep the flagstone in front of it.

"See you later. I'm headed to work. When he wakes up, tell him that I changed my mind. I don't want to talk," Angel whispered and eased out the back door.

———

Hilda counted to ten slowly, then went out to the front porch where Clancy was snoring loudly on the porch swing. So, this was the sorry bastard who'd caused her Angel to be single at the age of twenty-eight...who'd made her cry when she was younger, and who'd upset her today. He wasn't a bad-looking fellow—tall, well-built, dark hair, dark stubble starting to show on his face where he needed to shave.

Hilda loved Angel like a daughter, and it broke her heart to see her upset, especially on Sunday afternoons when she came home from her precious baby son's grave. She hooked the broom handle in the back of the swing and shoved with all her might.

One minute Clancy was dreaming of having the sweet angel he used to know in his arms beside the creek bank, and the next he was flying across the porch, grabbing at the air for something to hold on to. Then his eyes sprang open just in time to see the wooden floor as he landed facedown.

"Why did you do that?" he sputtered as he sat up.

"Me?" Hilda looked shocked.

The old green pickup he remembered from high school roared around the end of the house and out onto the dirt road headed west. "Where's she going?" He sat up, checking his nose to see if it was bleeding.

"I wouldn't know, you dirty scoundrel. She said to tell you that she'd changed her mind and she doesn't want to talk. You'd best haul your butt on out to that fancy car of yours and get out of here."

"Kept my promise," Hilda spoke to herself as she watched him leave.

Chapter 5

"Good mornin'," Patty greeted Angel when she opened the door to her office. "Have a good weekend?" She tossed her long, straight hair over her shoulder and opened another letter with a silver dagger.

"Had a helluva weekend." Angel took her sunglasses off, revealing red and swollen eyes. "I've cried buckets and buckets, and Hilda has used every cuss word she knows."

"What happened?" Patty's brown eyes were round as saucers.

"Call the rest of the girls for a meeting in my office," Angel said, adding, "Just us, not the rest of the board." She opened the heavy double doors into her private office and poured steaming hot coffee into a mug with the Conrad Oil Enterprises logo on the side. Bless Patty's heart, she was more than the best executive assistant in the world. She was also a good friend.

"Okay," the five of them said in unison as they sat down around the table. "What happened?"

"He followed me to the cemetery"—Angel leaned back and pinched the bridge of her nose with her finger and thumb—"and now he knows everything," she told them. "I should have closure, but I don't. I spent the whole weekend crying my stupid eyes out."

Angel looked around the table at the faithful friends who had stood by her all these years. They had come a long way since she'd met Allie in the university library ten years ago. Angel had been five months pregnant with Clancy's baby and working on a geology assignment. The two young women became instant friends. Before long, Allie had introduced her to the rest of the gang, and every one of them had cried with Angel when the baby was stillborn.

"Damn him!" Mindy swore. "Just when I thought I had you on the right track. Just when you were starting to do some serious dating. Why did he have to come back in the picture now? Lord, we haven't got time for this. We've got a wedding to plan for Bonnie and a divorce for me to get through, and Lord knows Susan is going to wake up someday and say yes to Richie. Seems like he asks her to marry him at least once a week."

"And I'm pregnant," Allie said bluntly. "Guess there ain't no time like the present to announce it. We seem to be having a group confession."

"Well, hallelujah." Angel smiled and her eyes began to twinkle. "I'm glad to hear that. You aren't goin' to quit work, are you?"

"Hell no. Next to you, I'm the best damn geologist in the great state of Texas, and I'm not even thinkin' about quitting work. I'll strap my baby on my back and tell those drillers how to do their jobs, and my kid can grow up knowing everything there is to know about oil wells," she said. "But what are you goin' to do if he comes back again? He knows where you live and where your company is," Allie said.

"I don't know. I thought it was all behind me. I thought I could go back to that alumni banquet, strut my stuff, show off the band, and leave feeling fine, but it didn't work that way. The minute I saw him, my insides turned to jelly and that old ache was right back in my heart," Angel told them. "I just wanted you all to know the situation up front. One part of me still wants to kiss him, and the other part wants to watch him die a slow and gruesome death."

"If you want to watch him die, I won't let him past my part of the building if he shows his face here." Susan gave her a thumbs-up. "Don't worry. First office is my territory. If he gets past me and my big old double-barreled shotgun, then Mindy can head him off at the pass."

"Sure." Mindy nodded. "I'm in a bad situation. You know, this divorce stuff is for the birds. I've decided sex is a misdemeanor. The more I miss, de meaner I get. Clancy Morgan better not try to sweet-talk his way past my office, or he'll find out he's dealin' with PMS and abstinence at the same time. Don't worry, we'll toss him out of the second-floor window on his handsome face, and then your insides won't turn to jelly when you look at him."

Angel laughed and shook her head. The whole Clancy Morgan thing had seemed like such a big mountain this morning, but the girls were whittling it down to the molehill that it really was. "You're good for me," she said. "Guess we better dry our tears and run this oil business now. The big boys would just love to see me blubbering over a lost love, wouldn't they? They said I'd never make it in a man's world, but I've got you all. Six of us can outdo the work of a hundred men."

"Hell, one of us can outdo that many," Patty swore. "We'll

manage, Angel. We've lived through marriages and rumors of marriages, war and peace, and I betcha this don't keep the sun from coming up either." Angel went back to her office and turned on her computer. It was time to get out of the rut she'd allowed herself to wallow in for the past two days and to get back to work. That's what she needed—good, complicated, exhausting work to erase Clancy Morgan's face from her mind.

By noon, she'd argued with the board of directors, had a meeting with Mindy concerning the wording on a multimillion-dollar contract, and met with Susan about advertising in *The Oklahoman*. The phone rang, and Patty answered, "Conrad Oil Enterprises. May I help you?"

"Whoops." She put her hand over the receiver and pressed the intercom button into Angel's office. "Guess Susan is out to lunch. Seems like the monster has gotten past her double-barreled shotgun."

"What?" Angel whispered back.

"It's Clancy on the phone," Patty said. "Want me to tell him to drop dead or that I'm putting a contract out on his hide? How about I tell him you've left for a month on your honeymoon?"

"I'll talk to him," Angel said. "I hope he's been as miserable as I have."

"Yeah, for a whole weekend," Patty said sarcastically. "That isn't ten years, you know."

Angel frowned at Patty and shut the door between their offices.

"Hello, Clancy. You do realize that this is called stalking. Am I going to have to put a restraining order on you?"

"Angela?" His voice sounded weary.

"Yes, this is Angel," she said.

"I owe you one hell of an apology. I'm so sorry. I'm miserable from it all, and I don't even know what to say. I've been a jackass and there's no excuse for what I did back then. I was just a scared kid and a jerk, and I deserve anything that you want to heap on me…"

"Am I supposed to forgive you?" she asked.

"I don't deserve your forgiveness, Angela," he said in a broken voice. "I don't deserve anything from you. I was prepared to meet a little kid that might look like me, or for you to tell me you'd given it away to a couple who couldn't have children. I would like to talk to you in person, and then I promise I'll get out of your life and never bother you again."

"Is that a real promise or one of those like you used to make?" she asked.

"It's real, and it's coming from a broken heart," he said. "Can I meet you or pick you up for dinner?"

"Sure," she said. "You can pick me up right here in my office at five o'clock this afternoon. But you'll have to be seen with me in public this time, since I don't think we've got time to go to Pennington Creek like we used to."

"I'll be there," he said tersely.

She punched the intercom and said, "Patty, tell Susan and all the girls to hold their fire. Clancy is coming at five o'clock, and I don't want a single shot in him when he gets to my office. I don't think even Hilda could get the blood out of these carpets. When he walks in, Susan is to meet him at the door and take him back down the hall... Mindy gets him there, and you know the rest. I want him to see every office and talk to every one of us before he gets up here. We're going to settle this thing, and somehow, I'm going to get him out of my life and my heart. When the sun comes up tomorrow, Clancy Morgan is going to be forgotten as far as I'm concerned."

Patty hid a smile. She'd be willing to bet her brand-new pickup truck against a wagonload of horse manure that by tomorrow Clancy would still be swaggering around looking like a million dollars, and by the end of the month, Angel would have a mended heart.

At five o'clock, Clancy pushed the door open to the first floor, and one of the members of the band met him with a fake smile plastered on her face. "Welcome to Conrad Oil Enterprises, Incorporated. My name is Susan. I'm in charge of PR and advertising. Maybe you remember me from the alumni concert we gave last week. I play the fiddle." She stuck out her hand and shook his firmly, hoping to intimidate him.

"Who died and left this company to Angela?" he asked bluntly.

"No one," Susan said. "Follow me, please. Angel is a top-notch geologist, and she knows as much about the oil business as anyone. She majored in geology and minored in business, and she's a hellcat on wheels when it comes to making deals. She played a hunch right out of college and drilled a well on the property she inherited from her grandmother. People all told her she was crazy. There wasn't any oil in that part of the state. But she ignored them and bet every last cent she had on that hunch. It paid off, and then she invested the money wisely, and in a few months, she owned her own company. When the Texanna Red Oil Company wanted to move their base to Louisiana, they offered to sell this building to her, and she bought it."

"Hello, Mr. Morgan." Mindy met him at the open door to her part of the building. "These are our directors' and lawyers' offices. Follow me, please. By the way, I want you to keep in mind that I could shoot you between the eyes and enjoy watching you die a slow and painful death," she said, in the same matter-of-fact tone she would've used to order a tuna-fish sandwich for lunch. "You've made Angel miserable and she's my best friend."

"I realize that, Mindy," he said. "Am I going to have to talk to everyone in Conrad Oil before I get to her?"

"Yup. That's the only way you get to the top in one piece and alive," she said. "Angel takes care of us all, and we take care of her. So, you better watch your step or I'll dream up some crazy lawsuit to bedevil you with," she added sweetly.

Clancy just nodded.

"Hello, Clancy." Allie met him at the top of the stairs on the second floor. "So, you're the infamous rich boy who—"

"Nice to meet you too." He gritted his teeth. "This is ridiculous."

"But necessary," Allie said firmly. "Shall we continue the tour? This is the geology department, where we decide when, if, and where to drill. Angel spends a lot of time here since she's the only geologist in the whole state of Texas who has better intuition than I do. There've been times when my call would have netted us a million dollars' worth of dry well. She's got a sixth sense when it comes to drilling. Too bad she doesn't have one when it comes to you."

He scowled but said nothing.

"Clancy Morgan, I do believe." Bonnie took over next. "I'm glad to finally meet you, and I think maybe I owe you a pat on the back. If you hadn't been such a rat to Angel ten years ago, not one of us would be where we are today. She's kept us together and we love her. So, say what you have to, then back out of her life."

"If I ever get to see her," he said flatly. "I didn't know I had to run the gauntlet to reach the top floor. I thought I'd just ask where she worked, get on an elevator, and find her office."

"Well, that's what you get for depending on your own shallow thinking," Bonnie said as she opened the door marked with a brass plaque that read ANGELA CONRAD, PRESIDENT. "Patty, he's all yours," she said.

"Clancy, you SOB, come right in here and sit down," Patty said with a big smile. "Angel is on the phone to a CEO in Maine, and she'll be a little while."

She closed her computer and sat down across from him. "Why did you treat her so rotten anyway?"

"Because I was a scared eighteen-year-old kid who thought the whole world was Tishomingo, Oklahoma. I was stupid enough to believe that what people thought about me would either make or break me," he said honestly. "I've listened to all of your opinions all the way up from the bottom. Now let me ask you something. Why in the hell did she make me meet every one of you?"

"Because every one of us was with her the night she gave birth to your son. We timed the contractions for her when she was in labor and held her hands when it was time to push. We were her cheerleading squad when the pains were so hard they took her breath away, and we cried with her when that little boy was stillborn. We all held him in our arms one by one and offered to kill you to make it up to her. She wouldn't let us do it.

"So, we just thought we'd get to know you, even though all she'll let us do now is walk with you from one office to the next. You might talk your way back into her life but if you make her cry again, you're going to disappear—just like that. Someone might find you in six million years when they drill for oil...but it'll probably be a dry hole like your cold old heart."

She broke off abruptly when Angel appeared in the doorway. "Clancy! Please come in."

After the treatment her girlfriends had put him through, Clancy was surprised to hear the genuine welcome in her voice. Patty threw him a warning look that Angel somehow missed and made herself scarce. Angel chattered on nervously as Clancy sat down by her desk.

"I've got a few loose ends to tie up here and then we can go to dinner. Do you still like Mexican food? I know a little place where they serve the real stuff, but the spices will fry your innards, so I hope you like it hot." She finished up, feeling a little foolish. "Did the girls give you the official tour of Conrad Oil?"

"They sure did. I was impressed."

"Wonderful bunch, aren't they?" She closed a folder and shut down her computer. "Met them my first semester in college. That's when we formed the band. Played the honky-tonks and dives in those days for extra money to help pay our way through school. Lord knows, I never would have made it through that first year without them. They were the first real friends I ever had, and we've stayed together through thick and thin, marriages and divorces, tears and giggles. There now, I think everything else can wait until tomorrow. Are you ready?"

"I'm ready." He smiled for the first time. "And I love Mexican. They can't make it too hot for this Okie."

"Elevator or stairs?" she asked as they passed Patty's desk.

"Elevator," he said bluntly. "I think I've had enough exercise for today."

They walked to the corner of the block in silence and into a small café. The waitress seated them at the back of the restaurant, at Angel's usual table.

"Margarita?" she asked.

"Iced tea for me." Angel unrolled the bandanna wrapped around the silver utensils and put it over her lap. "Clancy?"

"Iced tea is fine," he said.

"Now what do you want to talk about?" She picked up the menu and scanned it.

"Us. I still want to know what you've done these past ten years, even though your friends each filled me in a little," he said, then looked up at the waitress. "I'll have the chicken enchiladas. Do they come with refried beans and rice?"

"Yes, sir." The waitress nodded. "And a side order of hot vegetables and flour tortillas?" She turned to Angela.

"Bring me the beef fajitas, a full pound tonight. I'm hungry. And extra vegetables for an appetizer."

"Yes, ma'am," she said, and disappeared into the kitchen.

Angel looked right into Clancy's eyes and didn't blink. "I was hoping all your questions would be answered by now."

"How did you get started in the oil business?" he asked, ignoring her remark.

"When my great-grandfather died, he left us the farm, twenty acres of the prettiest green grass in the state. We left Tishomingo since we could live in Kemp rent-free and it was closer to Southeastern Oklahoma State University in Durant. They had given me a grant and a scholarship. Guess you forgot about me telling you that," she said. "Anyway, four years later Granny died, and I graduated with a major in geology and a minor in business right after I buried her. I had a hunch and drilled on the property. Everyone thought I was a fool, because there wasn't an oil well anywhere around Kemp, Oklahoma, but it turned out right, and I was pretty well off overnight. Then I played a few more hunches, and everything I touched turned to gold. The girls helped me a lot. Allie is a geologist, Mindy is a lawyer, and Bonnie is a wizard at accounting."

"And Susan is great at PR, and Patty is a top-notch assistant who would like to feed my heart to the buzzards," he finished for her.

"You can't blame them," she said, defending her friends.

"I guess not, if I'm telling the truth. And while we're being honest, I've got a couple of things to tell you. That night you told me you were pregnant, I wanted to sit down and promise you the moon, but my mother and father would have died if I'd come home and told them I'd gotten you pregnant. My friends were waiting at the Dairy Queen, celebrating the last night before we all left for college. Melissa was there, and she started flirting. I was so mixed up that I didn't know straight up from backward. Before long, we were dating, and we got married the week after we graduated from college. She taught school while I was in the air force. She didn't make my heart do backflips like you did, but we got along pretty good until one fine day when she announced she wanted a divorce so she could marry the principal at her school.

"I moved out, filed for divorce, and came home to Oklahoma as soon as my enlistment was up. I got my master's degree and a job teaching chemistry in Oklahoma City. I felt like I deserved what I got after the way I treated you that night. End of story. I tried my best not to think about you, Angel. I was a young, stupid fool who handled things wrong. I was too proud to stand up to my family or even to all of my friends and tell them that I was dating you all summer, much less admit that you were pregnant."

Angel's eyes shifted from one thing to another, never landing on him, but he had things to get off his chest, so he continued. "Melissa was the right girl from the right family who would know all the right things to say and do. It may be too much information, but she was cold in the bedroom, and sex was a bargaining tool, not something that was out of love. She didn't make me feel like a million dollars the way you always did. At first, I thought I just didn't know better because I'd only been with you and then her, but I've been with other women since then, and I learned better. They say you never forget your first love. Whoever said that was a genius, because it's the truth. I've never had the same almost euphoric feeling I had when we made love on the creek bank. Not even close."

She locked gazes with him, but her expression was unreadable.

Clancy wondered if he'd said too much, if maybe he'd done more harm than good with his admission. But the heaviness that he had carried around in his heart for years was gone, and he could breathe again without feeling as if his insides were twisted in a pretzel when he even thought about Angel.

"Well, enough soul cleansing," Angel said as the waitress

put the hot platters of food in front of them. "You know my story and now I know yours. But there isn't a future for us today, any more than there was that hot August night ten years ago. It's over, Clancy. We've both grown up, and we've changed drastically. I'm not that same little poor girl who fell in love with you, and you're not the person who was ashamed to be seen with me. It takes a good firm foundation to build a house, and a relationship is like that. Trust is the cornerstone, and I wouldn't trust you as far as I could throw you."

Chapter 6

On his way back to Tishomingo, Clancy stopped in Durant at a liquor store and bought two six-packs of beer and a pint of Jack Daniel's. Then he headed northwest, meaning to drown his sorrows, even if that was childish and not one damned thing would have been accomplished when the sun came up tomorrow morning. It had been years since he'd been drunk, and tonight he intended to get so plastered that by morning his head would feel like a drum was keeping time inside it and then maybe he wouldn't think about Angela.

He had been a complete fool to think that he would bare his heart and soul, and she would rush into his arms, tell him all was forgiven, and they'd ride off into the sunset to find their happily ever after.

"Hey, Clancy!" Meredith called from the kitchen when

she heard him open the door. "I had salad with the ladies at the country club. Have you eaten?"

"Yep." He nodded. "But I'm going out again to do a little fishing. Probably won't be back until morning."

"Okay. I've got to make phone calls about the auxiliary picnic next week." Meredith came into the living room. "I've got a hairdresser's appointment in the morning at nine, so please be quiet if you come in late." She smiled, showing beautiful white teeth. Meredith Morgan worked at keeping both her figure and her skin flawlessly young, and it was easy to see where Clancy had gotten his good looks.

He went down the hall to the bedroom that had been his since he was a baby. He changed from navy-blue pleated dress slacks and a pinstriped shirt into a pair of faded jeans and a faded tank top, kicked his good loafers in the floor of the closet, and pulled on a pair of grungy white tennis shoes with no laces. "See you later," he called as he left the same way he'd come in, noticing that his mother did take a moment to look up from the phone and wave at him.

He parked the Bronco near Pennington Creek, took an old blanket out of the back, and tucked it under his arm. Shuffling the beer and bourbon until they fit under his other arm, he plodded down the pathway to the sandbar. In the past ten years, the brambles had grown under the trees so much that he had to fight them to reach the very spot where he and Angel had lain together so many times. Tonight, there was nothing left, just as Angel had said, so he carefully spread out the blanket, scaring away a frog and a grass snake while he was at it. Then he picked up the first six-pack of beer, took off his shoes, rolled up the legs of his jeans, and stuck his feet in the water.

He popped the top on the first can and guzzled about half the contents before he came up for air. He hummed a few bars of a song until he remembered the lyrics...something about a man who had never been happy until he had a wife and kids. He tilted the can back and let the rest of the beer slide down his throat in one big swallow. Then he sang the rest of the lyrics at the top of his lungs, off-tune and off-key, just to make himself feel worse. He popped the tab on another silver can and continued to sing, until a sudden thought stopped him cold.

"I could've had a wife and kids," he whispered to himself. "But I threw it all away because of my pride and my fears. Well, here's to all the mistakes made by all the young, proud fools in the whole state of Oklahoma in the last ten years." Clancy opened the third can of beer and started sipping it slowly.

He had almost finished the first six-pack by eleven o'clock and his fishing equipment was still in the back of the Bronco. He lay on his back, his feet in the water and beer cans stacked in a crazy pyramid next to him, watched the moon rise, and thought of another song. He started to hum and whisper the words. "Try... Try... Hmm... Try to remember why we fell in love."

"Hello," a feminine voice said to his right.

"Angel?" He didn't even look. The sound of her voice was probably just a drunken illusion, but even if it were, maybe he could carry on a make-believe conversation with her.

"Who?" the voice asked, annoyed.

"Angel?" he repeated without taking his bleary eyes off the moon.

"Look at me, Clancy. God almighty, did you drink all these beers? What in the hell do you think you're doing? You're a grown man with a responsible job, and you've never been able to hold your liquor. Your high school principal would probably fire you on the spot if he knew you were lying down here in the dirt half-crocked and talking to the angels. Have you been smoking weed as well as drinking?"

He turned and looked at his ex-wife, Melissa, sitting on the sandbar beside him. "I'm not layin' in the dirt. I'm layin' on a blanket." Good God! What was she doing there? And was she real or just a figment of his drunken imagination? One thing for sure, she was right about him not being able to hold his liquor. That was the whole point. He was willing to fry a few brain cells to get the image of Angel out of his mind when she told him they could never build another relationship.

He chuckled.

"What's so funny? You have been into something other than beer, haven't you?" She popped her hands on her hips and glared at him.

"You being here is funnier than the time the preacher sat on the cake at the church social," he slurred.

He hadn't seen her in three years, not since their day in divorce court. What a helluva time for her to show up. He noticed a few wrinkles around her eyes, and her blond hair was shorter than he'd ever seen it. Other than that, she was the same old Melissa, looking as if she'd just walked out of *Vogue*. He impulsively looked down at her feet. Her toenails were freshly polished. How many times had he been ready to go somewhere and had to wait for Melissa's toenails to dry before they could leave?

"Your mother said you might be down here fishing," she said. "We need to talk."

"About what, Melissa?" he asked. "Talking with you is in the past. We're divorced, and why are you even in Tishomingo?"

"I come home every summer for a week to see Momma and Grandma, remember?" she said. "Since we got divorced, you've never been here when I am, and you're too drunk to remember anything about me anyway."

"Oh, I remember very well. You were all sexy until we got married, and then you were an icicle. Did your new husband figure that out too? Have a beer. Maybe it'll warm you up for him." He held up a full six-pack, still held together with the plastic webbing.

"You know I hate beer," she snarled.

"Then grab that bottle of bourbon under that tree bough, and we'll drink to the good old days." He laughed sarcastically.

"You really are drunk," she snarled again.

"And you're married," Clancy reminded her. "I'll get the damned bourbon. Never let it be said I was a bad host at my own self-pity party, even if you are an uninvited guest." He slurred the last word and wobbled just a little bit when he stood up. In his topsy-turvy world, the sandbar swirled, and the moon dropped about six feet toward the horizon, but he didn't fall.

"Here's the stuff." He staggered back to the blanket, flopped down, and stuck his wrinkled feet back in the water. Ignoring his ex-wife, he fell back to stare at the stars again. "Sorry, I can't give you a crystal glass to drink it out of. Just tip the bottle back and drink it straight."

"What's gotten into you? You never drank," she reminded him. "You always were the designated driver, even in the air force, and you wouldn't even drink a glass of wine with me on our first anniversary."

"You wouldn't understand." He worked hard to make his words come out right.

"Did I do this to you, Clancy?" she whispered.

He chuckled down deep. The chuckle soon became a laugh, and he sat up to wipe his eyes with the back of his hand.

"Oh, Clancy." She shook her head. "You were so brave through the divorce. I never knew I caused you this much grief. Have you been drinking ever since?"

"Hell no!" He raised his voice loud enough to be heard all the way across the creek.

"You poor man. I'm so sorry." She sighed, but he knew her. That was the sign for him to give in to whatever she wanted.

"You ought to be." Clancy sat up slightly, then fell back on his old blanket again. "You ought to be sorry because you never did love me. You never loved anybody but yourself, Melissha." He heard himself slur her name and made a mental note to work harder at keeping his words straight, because he damned sure intended to tell her what he thought about her while she was sitting there, acting like a soap opera star.

"Oh, Clancy, I did love you. I never really stopped loving you," she whined.

"None of that matters a whole helluva lot, now, Meliss...a." He was proud of himself for saying it just right. "Because I didn't love you either. I just married you because everyone thought that's what we should do. You had the wedding planned, and there were all those showers and presents, and I knew I'd be considered a real heel if I backed out of the marriage then. You know who I really loved? I loved Angela Conrad," he said.

"You're full of crap," she said. "You couldn't love her. She was a nerd, and she's probably off somewhere with a house full of snotty kids—"

"Angel owns Conrad Oil Enterprises in Denison, Texas," he said, as clearly as if he were stone-cold sober. "She's not a nerd and never was."

"Oh, she's Angel now, is she? Well, you didn't love her. You were in love with me from that time we all met at the Dairy Queen not long after graduation," she reminded him. "Remember how we flirted that night? You came in all sad and downhearted, and I cheered you up."

"I had just been a big jerk, and you were there." He shrugged.

"Sure." Melissa tucked a stray strand of hair behind her ear. "You had the senior blues. Graduation was over. Football season was done. College hadn't started. We were all scared of change. Why do you say you had been a jerk?"

Clancy didn't answer for a while. The six beers were wearing off faster than he thought they would, and he wasn't looking forward to the headache tomorrow morning—even if he did deserve it.

"That whole summer I was seeing Angela Conrad. I was mean to her that night, and I came to the Dairy Queen to hang out with all y'all." He shrugged again. "I was young and stupid and didn't realize that Angela was in love with me. Hell, I didn't even realize I was in love with her."

Melissa slapped him hard across the face, sobering him even more.

"Don't hit me again, Melissa," he warned in an icy

tone. "Don't ever hit me again. I'm just tellin' you what happened."

"You bastard." Melissa stood up and shook the sand off the bottom of her khaki walking shorts. "Were you thinking of her the whole time we were married?"

"Who were you thinking about when you were sleeping with the principal after we were married?" Clancy asked. "At least I wasn't committing adultery. Guess we're about even, for what it's worth."

"Shut up!" she said.

"Angela got pregnant," he said. "I came down here that hot August night a week before we were to go to college. I was going to tell her I wasn't coming back any more no matter what, and she told me she was pregnant with my child. Know what I told her? I didn't stand beside her and face the wrath of my parents. Oh no, I was the biggest chicken of all time. I told her to marry Billy Joe, and I walked away from her as if she was nothing to me."

"Why are you telling me this now?" Melissa asked.

"Because you need to know you're not the reason I'm trying to get drunk tonight," Clancy said. "I don't give a damn about you. I'm still in love with Angela—Angel—and she won't have a thing to do with me, because I ran out and left her. My son was stillborn, Melissa, and I didn't even care enough to find out until now."

"Goodbye, Clancy," she said. "I hope you rot in hell. Does your mother know this? She's always hoped you and I would get back together. So evidently, she hasn't got a clue. But she will tomorrow, Clancy. Because if you don't tell her, I will."

"Bet you would just love to do that, wouldn't you?" He laughed heartily. "Go ahead. Tell her. Go down to the weekly newspaper and put it on the front page for all I care. I love Angela Conrad. Always have and probably always will."

Melissa stomped off in the sand, got into her car, and laid down smoking rubber as she squealed the tires in anger. Clancy pulled his feet from the water and looked at the wrinkled skin while he finished sobering up. So much for getting drunk and singing sad songs tonight, or for shutting the door on his past failures and secrets. But what the hell? At least Melissa hadn't gone away with a lilt in her step, thinking he was still madly in love with her and he was corroding his liver to prove it.

━━━━━━━

He sat for hours, thinking about Angel, and then he gathered up his blanket, tossed the unopened bottle of bourbon in the back of the Bronco with the last six-pack of beer, and started back home to tell his mother what had happened. Tishomingo, like most small towns, had its own special gossip vine, and his mama didn't need to find out about his past at the beauty shop tomorrow morning.

"Hello, Clancy." An old movie was playing on late-night television when he crossed the living room and sat down in his dad's leather recliner next to his mother. She had on one of those mask things that made her face all green and cracked looking, and her hair was wrapped up in a towel. "Did Melissa find you? I told her you'd gone fishing. You know that girl comes to see me every year when she comes to visit her relatives. She says she still feels like I'm her mother-in-law. I think she regrets the way your marriage ended. I hope you aren't crazy enough to give her a second chance. She just got a divorce a few weeks ago, and she's always been one of those girls who needs a man around her to tell her how beautiful she is." She spoke without taking her eyes from the movie. "Good Lord," she finally noticed Clancy's feet. "What did you do? Fish barefoot in the water all evening?"

"Nope. I put my feet in the water and then I laid back and watched the moon come up. I tried my damnedest to get sloppy drunk, but it didn't work," he said honestly.

"Drunk?" Meredith's eyes widened out so much that the green mask cracked even more. "You?"

"Yep, me," he said. "Mother, I've got a confession. The summer after my senior year I was sneaking around with Angela Conrad..."

"Not Dotty Conrad's granddaughter," she gasped.

"Yes," he admitted. "I fell in love with her, but I was too young and stupid to realize it. Besides, I couldn't tell you and Dad."

"But why? Dotty might not have had money, but she was a fine woman. And Angela was probably the nicest little girl I ever met. Remember, Dotty used to clean house for me?" his mother whispered. "Angela came with her lots of times. But then maybe you didn't know that. You were usually out with your friends. Anyway, Angela didn't come with her after she was about sixteen. Dotty said she was cleaning somewhere else so they could make more money."

"Good grief, you mean Angela was hired help?" Clancy wiped a tear away from his eye.

"Sure. She dusted and ran the vacuum lots of times for Dotty when she was in junior high school, and then she went on to clean for some of my friends," Meredith answered.

"Mother, she was pregnant at the end of the summer after

high school," he said bluntly, "and I ran out on her. I was scared she'd embarrass me and you and Dad."

"You did what?" Meredith sat up straighter and gave him "the look."

Clancy suddenly felt two feet tall. Angela had been right about him, but now his mother was disappointed in him as well.

Meredith shook her finger at him. "I didn't raise you to be uncaring and selfish. You had a responsibility to that girl, and she was such a nice, sweet kid. Why didn't you tell me?"

He ducked his head like he did when he was a little boy and had done something he wasn't proud of. "I was ashamed, confused, and downright stupid."

"Do I have a grandchild?" she asked.

"No, my son was stillborn. I didn't find out about it until this week, and now I realize I'm still in love with Angela. Of course, she doesn't want anything to do with me!" he said miserably.

＝＝＝＝＝

Meredith Morgan had never seen her son so unhappy. Life could take some crazy twists. For weeks, she'd been worried about what everyone in town would say when they found out she'd begun dating again, and now the buzz at the beauty shop tomorrow morning would undoubtedly center on Clancy.

"Since you've been honest with me…" Meredith paused. "I've been seeing a man."

Clancy jerked his head around to stare at her. His mother knew that his dad had been right up there next to God in Clancy's eyes. Granted, his mama wasn't an old woman, but still the thought of her with someone else made him both sad and angry at the same time. He was speechless for several moments, and when he did try to say something, the words wouldn't come out of his mouth.

"You what?" If he had still been drunk, that would have sobered him right up. Finally, he got the courage to ask, "Who?"

"Tom Lloyd," she said.

"You're kidding me." He gulped.

"I'm quite serious," Meredith said.

"But, Mother, he's beneath you," he said. "He's—"

She nodded. "There is no one beneath me. We are all just people. And yes, I know that Tom's the maintenance supervisor at the cemetery. His wife died the same year your father did, and he's been lonely too. Clancy, I don't need money and I really don't give a damn about hanging around that fancy country club. That was your dad's scene, not mine. What I want is someone to love me and to spend time with me. I miss having a companion, Son."

Clancy's heart dropped. He didn't even know Tom, and he had judged him on a social basis. *Angel wouldn't have done that*, he thought.

He took a deep breath and asked, "When is he coming around so I can get better acquainted with him?"

Meredith patted his arm. "Guess you're more like me than I thought. Now, tell me, where again is it that Angela lives? And how did she get so rich as to own an oil company? Did you tell her that we used to own part of Texanna Red until your dad died and Red bought back the shares?"

He shook his head. "And I didn't tell her that Red wants me to work for him either. I don't love Conrad Oil. Like you said, I don't need money. I need Angel…and I've realized it too damned late!"

Chapter 7

PATTY TOOK ALL THE INCOMING CALLS, SO SHE KNEW CLANCY hadn't called Angel—at least not at the business. She had hoped that the trip to Tishomingo and the visit to the cemetery would bring closure to her friend, but it hadn't. Angel's green eyes were as sad as they had been the day they gathered around the black hole in the Kemp cemetery that was her grandmother's final resting place.

In Patty's opinion, the time had come for Angel to either kiss him or kill him and get on with life, and if no one else was going to prepare his wedding or his funeral, then Patty would take matters into her own hands—even if that made Angel mad. Facing her best friend's anger would be better than this damned cloud hanging over their heads while Angel went around sighing and declaring that she had buried all her memories and she was fine.

Patty crossed one long leg over the other one and tugged down the bottom of a lemon-yellow skirt. She took a deep breath and dialed the number that she had stolen from Angel's phone.

"Hello?" Clancy said.

"This is Patty at Conrad Oil," she said.

"Is Angel all right?" His voice sounded both worried and downright sad.

"She's fine physically, but not so good emotionally," Patty said.

"I know the feeling." Clancy said in a deep Texas drawl.

"Y'all need to get this worked out," Patty said.

"I agree, but I have no idea where to start, or what to do," Clancy said.

"I'll be in touch as soon as we have a plan," Patty said.

"I'm leaving soon on a short trip to Florida. I'm going down there for a few days. Maybe a few days on the beach will help me clear my mind. At least, that's what I'm hoping, but I'm not sure anything can do that." Clancy sighed.

"Where in Florida? We might be able to work with that." Patty's mind started racing in circles as she made a plan that could get her fired for sure.

"To a little hotel right on the beach west of Panama City Beach," he answered.

"I'll call you by the end of today," she said.

"Thank you, but why would you do this for me?" Clancy asked.

"It's not for you, believe me." Patty ended the call, checked the day planner, and found that Angel would be on a phone call with Tex from Texanna Red Oil Company in thirty minutes, then texted all the girls except Angel: *Mayday. Thirty minutes. Conference room.* When she swung the door open to the long, narrow conference room thirty minutes later, the others were already gathered around the table.

"What's up?" Allie looked a little green above her upper lip. "I swear, if morning sickness doesn't stop in a few weeks, this is going to be an only child. If Tyler wants to have a big family, he can have the rest of them." She rolled her eyes at the chocolate chip cookies on the table. "Where's Angel?"

"She's talking to Red and Anna about the move they're about to make. Red would like to talk her out of this building. Says his crew hates Louisiana and wants to come home to Texas," Patty said. "Sit down and let's make a decision. We don't have all day. We all know Angel is out of it these days. Lord, I can't work with her in this weird mood another day. It's like living with a zombie. I vote we send her on a vacation."

"Sure." Susan ran her hands through her short hair and laughed. "But Angel doesn't do vacations. It'd be easier to set up a snow-cone stand in hell than to talk her into taking time off."

"We could run the company without her for a little while, but she'll never agree to a trip." Bonnie did a *rat-a-tat-tat* on the table with her long fingernails. "You got something in mind, Patty?"

"Well, I do," Mindy butted in. "I vote we give her two weeks off for an early birthday present. She'll be twenty-eight at the end of the month and we've retired the band, so there's no reason she can't go. Now, where were you thinkin' about sending her, Patty?"

Patty smiled, and her eyes twinkled with excitement. "Panama City Beach, Florida. I know it's not as fancy as New Orleans or Paris, France, but it's a nice calm place with a little hotel that sits right on the sand. Remember when Ronald and I were dating and went there for a weekend? It was wonderful, and so quiet."

"Sounds like a great place for two people to fall in love all over again." Allie giggled. "I hope to hell Angel can't see through you as well as I can."

Patty gave them all an innocent look. "Me? Why, I just thought our dear friend needed to relax. But not by herself." She smiled. "Suppose a tall, handsome fellow who filled out his jeans real well, and who just happens to know her from high school… What if he happened to show up on the beach at the same time she did? Angel couldn't blame me for that, now could she?"

"And it's time she took him back or set him free—or else set herself free, which would be even better," Allie said. "She'll be here in a few minutes. Let's take her to dinner and tell her it's a done deal. You get the plane tickets and plans made, Patty."

"I'll do it," Bonnie said. "I can have everything ready at six o'clock. Let's go out for Italian food and tell Angel she can have tomorrow to get things packed and ready. She can fly out of Dallas Wednesday morning, and we'll even let her take a laptop. But she can only call in once a day unless it's a dire emergency. Who's informing Clancy?"

"Not me," Susan said. "I'm no good at tellin' lies or keepin' secrets."

"Well, this is too important to leave to amateurs," Allie said.

Bonnie raised her hand. "I'll call him, and then if she ever finds out, I'll blame it on Red. And I can keep a straight face when I lie. After all, I deal with the IRS."

All four women turned to look at her with raised eyebrows.

Bonnie shrugged. "And I did a little research and found out Clancy's father was in the oil business with Red at one time."

"Why are we doing this?" Allie asked. "We've wanted to shoot Clancy dead for ten years and now here we are, making arrangements to tell him where Angel is for two weeks. Not one damned bit of this makes a whole lot of sense to me."

"Angel's not happy," Patty said. "And the only thing that's goin' to make her happy is getting him either out of, or into, her heart. It's a love-him-or-leave-him kind of situation. So, we're just helping her get her life straightened out so we can get on with ours. We've got a baby to birth in a few months, a wedding to stage, and a divorce to finalize. We need to get Angel's love life back on track, so we can do all that and run this oil business like we need to do."

"I second the motion," Susan said. "Let's all agree before anyone chickens out. Meeting adjourned. See you all later." She passed the window looking down on Main Street as she moved toward the door. "Here she comes down the hallway. Better look sharp now and get back to work."

At five thirty, Angel got into the elevator, pushed the button for the first floor, and found all her friends waiting in the lobby.

They chatted about Red coming back to Texas and how they were glad Angel hadn't caved and sold him their office spaces. When they reached the Italian restaurant on the other end of the block, the waitress seated them at the back and brought a menu. There was something about the way the other five kept exchanging long looks that told Angel something was going on. She looked at Susan's face first, knowing full well her friend couldn't keep a secret in a bucket with a lid on it. She shifted her focus over to Patty to find her eyes were twinkling, and just as Angel shifted her gaze to Mindy, she caught her winking at Allie. Bonnie was the only one who didn't act as if she were sitting on a keg of dynamite with a short fuse.

Angel pursed her lips and said, "Okay. 'Fess up. What's going on?"

Bonnie produced a big yellow envelope and they all yelled, "Surprise!"

"We've got an early birthday present for you. Lord knows you deserve it, but you wouldn't think of doing it for yourself, so we bought it for you. You're going to Panama City Beach, Florida, for two weeks, to a beachfront motel. Your room has a balcony where you can sit out and listen to the ocean waves come in and smell the salty air. When you get bored with that, you can put on your bathing suit, sink your toes in the warm sand, and lay out on the beach until some knight in shining armor comes racing down the beach on his big white four-wheeler and steals your heart away. But remember, it's only for two weeks. If he wants you to run off to a castle in France, the answer is no, because at the end of that time, you've got to come back to Conrad Oil and go back to work!"

Angel's eyes misted. That they were thinking of her was so sweet, but she did not intend to leave her business or her friends for two weeks.

"You're all sweethearts." She unfolded the napkin at her fingertips and dabbed at the tears, leaving a black mascara smudge on it. "But the answer is no. I can't stand to be away from you all for that long."

"Bull," Patty said. "And we didn't ask a question so you can't answer no. You're goin' to be on that plane if I have to hog-tie you and hire some beach bum that looks just like Kenny Chesney to throw your body over his shoulder and put you in the plane seat."

"You know how much I like Kenny's singing, but the answer is still no," Angel argued.

"You need to unwind. There are plane tickets and reservations for the motel, and I took your business papers out of your briefcase and put in three trashy romance novels. You're goin' home tonight to pack, and we don't want to see your face at the office until two weeks from Wednesday. I'll even drive you to the airport," Patty told her. "Everything's taken care of."

Bonnie slid the envelope with the plane tickets across the table. "Happy birthday, Angel. Go down there and find a handsome guy to make your eyes sparkle and your heart float. You've got all the money you'll ever need, so you don't have to look for a rich man."

"Thanks a lot." Angel sighed. There was no getting out of it, so she might as well accept their offer. She'd flown all over the United States and abroad but had never dreamed of doing anything this self-indulgent. Lie on a beach somewhere with a trashy book and read to her heart's content?

She started to refuse—just one more time. "Now, you know I love you all—"

"Good," Allie butted in. "That's all the thanks we need to hear. I vote we order a bottle of sparkling wine to celebrate. I can't drink it, but I can enjoy watching y'all have a glass. And I'll be taking time off when this baby is born, and I betcha Bonnie's going to ask for a couple of weeks off for a honeymoon soon, so right now it's your turn, Angel, and you can't say no. We love you too."

Angel decided to give up arguing. She reached for the envelope and promised herself she would indulge her well-meaning friends and go—but she'd only stay until Sunday and fly back home in time for work on Monday morning.

"Okay, okay. You're all wonderful, and I guess you won't let me refuse," she said ruefully. "Just tell me that my new gorgeous beach bum will look just like Kenny Chesney. Y'all know how much I love him."

"None of that matters. He just has to worship you like you're a goddess," Bonnie said and picked up the menu. "I'm starving. I think I'll have the lasagna, and to hell with my diet for tonight. I may eat fried ice cream afterward too."

"Hear, hear!" Allie raised her water glass in a toast. "I'm eating for two even if y'all can't tell yet. So, I'm having baked ziti and hot bread, and I hope it doesn't come right back up!"

Angel's hunch wasn't satisfied. Something still wasn't right with this picture. She and her friends never kept secrets from each other, and yet Susan's expression told her there was something she still wasn't telling. Why did they want her out of the office for two weeks?

———————

It was after midnight when Patty called Clancy. The phone rang five times before a woman answered in a sleepy voice.

Anger began to boil up in the depths of Patty's heart and soul. How dare he pretend to love Angel and then spend the night with another woman? "I need to speak to Clancy," Patty said through clenched teeth.

"Who is this?" the woman asked. "Do you realize it's midnight?"

"Yes, ma'am," Patty said, "but I still need to talk to Clancy. This phone call involves Angel Conrad?"

The woman's tone changed. "Has something happened to Angela?"

"No, ma'am," Patty said.

"Just a minute. I'll take his phone to him," the lady said.

Patty heard the woman walking across a floor and saying, "Some woman wants to talk to you, Son."

"Oh!" A heavy weight lifted from Patty's heart. Clancy must be staying with his folks.

A few moments later, Clancy answered the phone. "Hello. Did your plan work?"

"Yes, but it took some fancy work, so you better appreciate it. Angel is flying to Panama City, and a car will deliver her to the Sugar Sands by the Sea. The rest is up to you," she said. "Get a pencil and take down this information. She'll fly out of Dallas on Wednesday morning at seven. Got that?"

"I still can't believe you are doing this for me," Clancy said.

"We want her back—with you if that's what it takes to make her happy. Or without you, if she can shake you out of her heart once and for all. But all you've got is two weeks, and what happens is up to you. We don't really give a damn about *you*, Clancy. We just want Angel to be happy, and we think this is the only way we can make that happen," Patty said. "And if you tell her about this call, I'll swear you're lying. And I don't have to tell you which one of us she'll believe."

"Thanks," Clancy said. "I'll catch a plane out of Oklahoma City on Wednesday morning, and I'll call for reservations in a nearby hotel. And believe me, I'll do my best."

"Two weeks, Clancy. That's all you've got." Patty hung up the phone and sent up a prayer that she was doing the right thing.

Chapter 8

Angel refused to have a car deliver her to the hotel, instead renting a vehicle so she could get around the area. She drove to the Sugar Sands and parked her car in front of the hotel.

The sky was pure blue, and there wasn't a single white cloud drifting over the water. The sand was as white as a new bride's veil, and right then, she was glad she had agreed to a few days away from work, stress, and thoughts of Clancy. She was going to lie on the beach until dark, then soak in the hot tub and read one of the trashy books Patty put in her briefcase from beginning to end.

"Hello," she greeted the man behind the desk. "I'm Angel Conrad, and I've got reservations for the next couple of weeks."

"That's right." He smiled. "Room 214, a corner room on the second floor with a nice view of the ocean. Enjoy your stay." He handed her the key and motioned to the colorful advertising flyers lined up neatly on the east wall. "Let us know if you'd like information about local attractions."

"Thank you." Angel took the key but didn't stop to pick up any brochures. Playing miniature golf or renting a sailboat wasn't what this vacation was all about. She was here to say her goodbyes to memories that had haunted her for ten years. Before she left this place on Sunday night, she planned to stand barefoot in the sand and let go of anything that reminded her even remotely of Clancy Morgan. Evidently, she'd been guilty of wearing her heart on her sleeve these past days and her friends had realized she needed some time to straighten out her life. Well, it *would* be straight come Monday morning, and they would never have to worry about her again.

Angel ignored the elevator, climbed the stairs to room 214, and opened the door. The suite was far more room than she needed, but she appreciated her friends getting her what was probably the best. She plopped the suitcase down on the bed, then went back down to the car for the rest of her luggage. The office door was open when she returned, and someone else was at the desk. She could hear the clerk telling him the same things he'd just told her with the same intonation, the same smile, the same wave of the hand. The new guest looked vaguely familiar from the back, but she shrugged. She certainly didn't know anyone in Florida.

She opted for the elevator that time, then kicked the unlocked door open with her foot and set her luggage on the floor. She opened the door to the bathroom and turned on the hot water, shucked out of her clothes, and took a long shower to ease the tension out of her muscles. When she finished, she wrapped herself in a big white towel and collapsed on top of the white duvet that covered the second queen-size bed and sighed. She propped up on both pillows and grabbed her cell phone to call Patty, but she changed her mind and tossed the phone to the other side of the bed. This was supposed to be a vacation, and she'd vowed on the plane that she would not call Conrad Oil once in the five days she planned to stay in Florida—instead of the two weeks her friends had expected her to be away.

She closed her eyes but couldn't sleep, so she got out of bed and opened one of her suitcases. She'd packed too much, but she had never been on a personal vacation and wasn't sure what she might need. She found her bright-red bathing suit, a white terry cover-up, and a pair of white leather thong sandals.

"I didn't come to the beach to hole up in a room," she declared. "Maybe that hunky beach bum who looks like Kenny Chesney is out there waiting for me."

She smiled as she imagined a tale to entertain the girls about a gorgeous man she'd met on the beach.

She had the doorknob in her hand and was about to turn it when a loud knock on the other side startled her. She jerked the door open to find a tanned young man with a smile that would make Patty swoon holding a gorgeous flower arrangement in his hands.

"Delivery for Miss Conrad," he said and handed her a crystal vase with a dozen red roses interspersed with white baby's breath. "Have a nice day now and don't forget your sunblock. Fair as you are, you'd burn in an hour on a day like this."

"Those girls!" Angel sighed as she set the flowers on the bar separating the living area from the kitchen. Then she opened the envelope attached to the red satin bow around the vase.

Yesterday, today, forever. The card wasn't signed.

"Well," she said aloud. "Allie always was one for

mystery. Probably trying to make me think there's someone here who's after my heart. Maybe he'll be a dark-eyed, gorgeous model who can wiggle out of a tight Speedo so fast he'll make my head swim." She picked up her tube of sunblock, threw it into her beach bag, stopped long enough to inhale the fragrance of the roses, and headed out the door to the beach.

Once there, Angel dropped her bag on the warm sand and took out an oversize towel. This end of the beach was quiet, and the sand was as fine and white as granulated sugar. She sat down on the towel and scooped up a handful, letting it slip through her fingers. Then she remembered the delivery boy's warning and dusted the fine grains from her hands, slid her sheer cover-up off her shoulders, and smoothed sunblock cream over her arms and legs.

A picture of the two entwined hearts she had drawn in the sand at the edge of Pennington Creek in Tishomingo ten years ago popped into her mind. Using her finger, she drew two hearts in the sand beside her beach towel. This time they weren't even touching.

She rolled over on her stomach and took one of the romance novels out of her bag. A picture of a handsome cowboy in tight jeans and a gaudy western shirt decorated the front. A woman with improbably deep cleavage was draped over his arm, and the smoldering look in his eyes promised the reader a love story beyond all expectations. Patty probably didn't even know the author and had picked it for the cover art. But whether the author could write or not didn't matter one bit to Angela. She intended to read the book from prologue to epilogue and enjoy every overheated page just to keep the thoughts of Clancy at bay.

Clancy changed into swimming trunks and put on a tank top and a pair of sandals. He threw a towel over his shoulder, took a deep breath, and started toward the beach. He had planned to just take a walk and clear his mind. He'd been able to get a room in the same hotel, found out which room Angel was in, and deliberately booked his room in the second tower on the third floor. He hadn't expected to see Angel so quickly. He hadn't even figured out how to approach her, but there she was, wearing a red two-piece bathing suit, a floppy straw hat, and huge sunglasses, propped up on her elbows reading a paperback book. But he would have known her if she'd been decked out in a gunnysack tied up in the middle with a length of twine. A young man strolled past her, and

Clancy could tell by his posturing and the way he slowed down that if she had looked up, the guy would've started a conversation, but she seemed to be oblivious to everything except the book.

"I guess there's no time like the present," he whispered as he flipped his towel out right beside her and sat on it, looking out over the ocean.

———————

It took Angel a moment before she realized Clancy was sitting beside her, but there was the same tightness in her chest and a catch in her breathing that she'd had when he showed up at the dam back when they were teenagers. She jerked off her sunglasses and looked right into Clancy's eyes. And all the pieces of the puzzle tumbled into place. She couldn't decide whether to fire her friends and watch them starve to death or simply shoot them and get it over with quickly. But one thing was for sure: when she got back, every one of them would be facing her wrath, and it wasn't going to be a pretty sight. All five were going to see her breathe fire before Monday morning was over.

"Small world, isn't it?" Clancy flashed a bright smile.

"Which one of them called you and told you I was here?"

She reached over and smudged the two hearts. She was here for closure, not to reunite with her old flame.

"Don't know what you're talking about." He didn't blink, but there was a twinkle in his eyes that made her heart flutter even more.

"Yes, you do." Angel was so mad she could have chewed up driftwood and spit out toothpicks. She quickly gathered her things and stuffed them into the beach bag. "I'm checking out of the motel right now and driving my rental car back to the airport. I'll be home by morning and my so-called friends will be facing the firing squad."

"Sit down, Angel." He patted the towel before she could yank it up. "You can't run from me forever. Stay and get to know me. I'm a man now, not the scared young boy who didn't know his own heart. I come down here for a few days in the summer every year, just to relax. Please give me a chance to show you that I've changed from that young stupid boy who walked out on you. Let me show you around town, and then, when we go home, if you don't ever want to see me again, I'll stay away."

She glared at him. "Did you send the roses?"

"No, I didn't send flowers." He shook his head. "I wouldn't do that or be here either, since you accused me of stalking, but your friends think we need to get this thing between us settled, and if we don't, neither of us can ever really move forward with our lives."

"All right, then." She nodded. "You've never lied to me, so I believe you." She plopped back down, not because he told her to, but because she'd be damned if she let his presence run her away.

"Thank you for that," he said.

They sat in silence for a full five minutes, and then her phone rang. Expecting it to be Patty, she had a fiery speech ready, but it was her old friend Red.

"Good mornin', Red," she said.

"You ready to let me buy you out, or else at least sell me back the building you're in?" he asked. "I'm willing to give you fifty percent more than you paid me for it."

"Not in your wildest dreams," she answered.

"Then I guess I'd better go lookin' for another building." He sighed. "Hey, I hear that you and my friend Clancy are taking a little vacation together."

"Not together, but at the same time and place, thanks to my best friends," she told him.

"I'll give you until you get home to make a decision about selling to me." He chuckled. "You and Clancy have a good time. Don't do anything I wouldn't do."

"That leaves me a broad range, now doesn't it?" Angel smiled. "So you know Clancy?"

"I hope so." Red chuckled. "Ask Clancy about our history if you want to know. Bye, now." He ended the call.

She laid the phone beside her and turned to Clancy. "That was Red. Just how do you know him, anyway?"

"He grew up in Milburn and was my dad's best friend. Dad owned a chunk of stock in Texanna Red Oil Company. He's been after me for years to come work for him instead of teaching high school," Clancy answered.

"He knew we were both in Florida. Is he in on this too?" Angel asked. "Did he tell you where I was?"

"No, he's not in on it, but I imagine he and your girls have been talking," Clancy answered. "But I don't mind who knows that we're here for a couple of weeks."

"Anyway, *you're* here for two weeks, but I'm on my way out of this place as soon as I can pack. Won't be too hard because I haven't really unpacked," Angel told him. "I came here to clear my mind, not to make more mistakes."

"Just let me take you to dinner and show you around the place for a couple of days, please. I've been here before. I know where all the good restaurants and the fun places to go are," he begged.

Angel had faced a pregnancy without a husband. She had worked like a dog to get an education. She had carved an oil business out of a hunch. She had buried the last living relative she had and helped her friends through so many hard times she couldn't count them on her fingers and toes.

She had never run from anything in her life, but she sure wanted to light a shuck, as her grandmother used to say, out of Florida right then. Still, maybe spending time with him would be the answer. Trying to ignore him sure hadn't worked.

"All right, dinner, but I bet when this vacation is over, it'll be *you* who'll be in a hurry to get back, Clancy," Angel said.

She found her book in the bag and threw the tube of sunblock lotion at him. "You might be tanner than me, but you'll still burn in sun like this. Help yourself. If you get a sunburn, I'm not going to play nurse for you." She flipped the romance novel open to the page where she had been reading and began to read—or, at least, try to read.

"I can't reach my back, and it looks to me like you didn't get enough on your shoulders. Do you think we could call a truce long enough to help each other out?" he asked.

"Why not?" she said indifferently. She closed her eyes

and remembered those two hearts drawn in the sand with *baby* written on the overlapping part. Her life had been shattered when she told him her secret that night, but by the end of two weeks, she might be over Clancy Morgan once and for all. That would sure be worth sticking around the beach the entire time for. Granny used to say the way to not crave chocolate bars was to eat them until you got so sick you upchucked. Angel changed her plan to fly home on Monday to staying for two weeks. She would spend so much time with Clancy that she would be sick of him in the next few days.

"Yes, ma'am. I'll do your back first." He squeezed the lotion into his big hands and gently rubbed her shoulders and down her back to where her bathing-suit top fastened.

She bit back a gasp when his hands made contact with her bare skin. Sparks that rivaled a fireworks show on the Fourth of July flitted around them, and the chemistry between them was just as strong as ever. No man had ever made her feel what Clancy had, and no one else's touch had ever make her heart flutter like this. Not that she had any immediate plans to tell him so—or any future plans for that matter.

"Want me to undo this snap and get your whole back, or just reach under it?" he asked, trying hard to keep his voice emotionless so she wouldn't know how just the feel of her skin affected him.

"Undo it," she said, hoping he didn't hear the breathlessness in her voice. Let him cope with his hormones however he could. Turnabout was fair play—another of her grandmother's sayings—and she was having enough trouble with the emotional roller coaster she was on.

"All done." He finished slathering lotion over every inch of her bare skin and refastened her top. "Your turn."

Angel rolled over and took the tube of sunblock from him. She braced herself for the jolt she expected when she rubbed lotion on his muscled back and legs. She walked on her knees until she was behind him, glad he couldn't see her eyes behind the sunglasses or hear the thumping of her heart over the sound of the ocean.

"Be still," she ordered when he turned his head to the left and locked eyes with her. She blinked and concentrated on his broad back and tight muscles. "What do you intend to do for two whole weeks? What does this place have to offer that will take all of two weeks to see?" Her voice sounded breathless in her own ears.

"Oh, honey, we could stay here a month and still not see and do everything they have around these parts. We can take a

boat trip out to Shell Island. We can do some deep-sea fishing."
Clancy said. "Or maybe I'll just lay right here and let you rub
lotion on me for two weeks. I want to spend time with you,
Angel, and get to know you all over again. I don't care about
seeing the tourist sights, but I'll go anywhere you want to. "

Angel slapped his shoulder. "Oh, hush. It'll take longer
than two weeks to get to know me. I'm not that naive teenager who thought you hung the moon and stars. I don't have
a trusting heart anymore."

"Hey," he said. "You knew what you wanted when
I didn't. I think you missed a spot over there on my right
shoulder. If I get a sunburn, you'll have to put up with my
whining," he teased.

"Heaven forbid!" She rubbed more sunblock on his shoulder. "Now lie down and take a nap, or I can give you a big,
thick romance novel to read. Sorry I don't have anything else
to offer. My dear friends didn't think to send along a thriller."

"A nap sounds wonderful. Don't leave without waking
me, though. I thought we'd have dinner at a seafood restaurant that I like, and then we'd play a round of miniature golf,
and after that we'd get a bottle of wine and come back here to
watch the tide come in." He crossed his arms above his head
and rested his face on the backs of his hands.

"Did Patty plan all that too?" she asked.

"Nope," he mumbled and closed his eyes.

Angel stared at the words in her book but she didn't see them. She alternated between waves of annoyance and sheer fear. She was still annoyed at her friends for pulling such a stunt, but she was scared to admit that she still had feelings for Clancy—and they weren't anger. She was as strong and independent as the heroine in the book she was reading. She could spend two weeks with Clancy and then walk away from him without a glance over her shoulder—at least that's what she told herself. But her heart disagreed.

Sparks continued to flit around her like fireflies on a spring night. Flutters in her stomach felt like dozens of butterflies all circling around a bonfire, knowing if they got too close they would get burned but wanting to feel the warmth of the blaze.

I got over him once before. I can do it again, she thought.

No, you didn't. Her grandmother's voice was loud and clear in her head. *You've never gotten over that boy, and I'm not sure you ever will.*

Just watch me, Angel argued.

She listened intently, but her grandmother had nothing more to say.

"Stop it!" Angel whispered aloud.

"Stop what?" Clancy's eyes popped open.

"I'm talking to my book," she lied.

"Oh." He smiled. "By the way, do the rules say I can't look at you?"

"I didn't make the rules. You and my so-called best friends did," Angel said tartly, turning the page she hadn't read. "I might warn you. I'm damned good at miniature golf, and I shoot a mean game of pool too. Used to pick up a few dollars on bets in the student union during college days. No one would believe a woman could outshoot those big, tough cowboys."

"Then we'll have to play pool before we leave here," he promised. "Have I told you in the last five minutes how gorgeous your eyes are when you're angry? They have flecks in them that glitter and glow."

"You can't see my eyes. I have on sunglasses," she pointed out.

"I can see your eyes anytime I want. I can see your body next to mine right now with my eyes closed. Both of them are forever branded into my thoughts. But I've got to admit, it's a lot better when you are really here beside me, Angela. Being with you right now is the most peaceful thing I've experienced in a long time. No matter what we're doing, I just want to be with you." Clancy kissed her gently on the cheek, then laid his head back down and shut his eyes.

Chapter 9

ANGEL GRABBED THE HEM OF THE FULL SKIRT OF A RED-AND-white-checked strapless sundress and drew a portion of it through a white plastic loop, showing off her left leg to the top of her thigh. She pulled her curls behind her ears with two long barrettes, slapped on a little bit of makeup, and buckled a pair of white leather sandals on her feet. She was dabbing perfume behind her knees and ears when she heard his knock on the door.

She left the bathroom and threw open the door that led onto the landing. Just looking at him standing there in khaki slacks and a light-blue button-down shirt put another case of flutters in her heart.

"You look lovely." His deep voice was even more husky than usual.

"Thank you, sir. You don't look so bad yourself." The top two buttons of his shirt were left undone, showing a thicker tuft of soft, dark-brown hair than he'd had ten years ago... and he smelled like heaven.

"Are you ready?"

She nodded and picked up her purse. He escorted her to the elevator and out to a silver Cadillac where he opened the door for her. Then he whistled as he walked around the car and settled in behind the wheel. He plugged his phone into a jack and tapped the screen. The Judds began singing one of the songs that her band had performed at the alumni reunion. "They aren't as good as you are," he said as he backed the car out and started driving east toward the restaurant where he had made reservations.

"Oh, sure," she argued. "The Judds are in Nashville making millions, and I've sold my bus and broken up my band. You've got rocks for brains if you think I'm that good."

"Then I've got rocks for brains. You're making millions, too, and they still can't sing as well as you. Remember when you used to harmonize with whoever was on the radio in my Camaro? I remembered that when I looked up there at that stage. You were standing there like an angel appearing out of a cloud of smoke. Lord, I thought I'd die when I realized it was you. When you hopped up there on the table in front of me, my mouth felt like it was plumb full of cotton. I wanted to say something, but words wouldn't come out of my mouth. Why didn't you give us all some advance notice of what you've accomplished?" he asked.

"I didn't need to advertise my success to all those people who never thought I'd amount to anything. Come on, Clancy. I was poor, but I wasn't dumb—except when it came to you," she told him. "Now where's this restaurant? I always get hungry when I'm around water very long. You know, I think this sunblock lotion really does work. I'm not burned at all," she rambled on, changing the subject.

Clancy pulled the car up to a restaurant with an awning in front. He handed a valet the keys and opened the door for Angela. "I figured you'd marry Billy Joe. You should have seen my face when I read that he was gay. Goes to show how much I knew, huh?"

The waiter showed them to a table for two on a wharf overlooking the water. A salty breeze blew the linen table-cloths and caused the candles, set down in deep crystal sconces, to flicker.

"Nice place," she commented when the waiter brought two tall glasses of iced tea and left with their orders. He ordered the steak and shrimp special, and she ordered a crab salad, with a side order of fried clams and shrimp with red sauce.

"Best I could do on short notice. I'll see if I can come up with something a little more elaborate for tomorrow night. There's a dinner cruise aboard a ship that goes out to Shell Island, but it was fully booked tonight. We can go another time. Takes most of the afternoon, then we'll eat dinner and spend an hour on an island before we return. Sounded kind of romantic. Then there's another restaurant the clerk said was good that I thought we'd try too. Unless, of course, you want to decide..."

Angel looked out at the setting sun's reflection on the water and thought she could probably come to this place every night for two weeks. Even if Clancy decided where they would eat every night, they'd probably still get on their separate airplanes to go back to Oklahoma. If at the end of their time Clancy Morgan asked her to go to Tishomingo and eat at the Dairy Queen in front of all his hometown friends, she would be really impressed.

"Surprise me," Angel said without looking at him. Two dolphins arched up out of the ocean and made graceful dives back into the water. "Did you see that?" she gasped. "It was absolutely beautiful."

"Not as beautiful as you," he said honestly, having a hard time taking his eyes from her bare shoulders and graceful neck. He would love to nuzzle in the softness below her ear, but he knew it would take several days before he could even begin to think in terms of a physical relationship, no matter how badly he wanted to feel her warmth next to him. Hell, he might finish two weeks of heartache and long, cold showers, then fly back to Oklahoma without a single kiss. The only thing Patty had promised was two weeks; she hadn't seemed to be promising any miracle.

"You're blind," Angel snorted.

Clancy looked like he might reach across the table to touch her hand but then drew back.

Angel turned her head back to the sunset and the water. *What would they talk about for two whole weeks?* Clancy wondered.

He would be content just to spend time with her, but she deserved a vacation. They'd shared something special ten years ago, but how could two adults build even a temporary relationship on the past?

He had known that she wanted more than just waiting for him at the creek. He would drive up, get out of his car, and find her right there, no questions asked, and they would make love under the tree branches. Afterward they usually went skinny-dipping in the warm water, sometimes to return for another session of insatiable teenage sex, sometimes to dry off and go home. He would drive her home, always by the back roads but never down Main Street, because someone might see him with her and report it all back to his folks.

"Penny for your thoughts." He dug in the pocket of his slacks and put a shiny copper penny at her fingertips.

"Cost you more than that." She cocked her head to the side in a gesture that had always been endearing to him. "You better eat hearty and get ready for the big golf match, because you're goin' to lose. And did you already buy wine? If not, get two bottles, because I really like good wine."

"I'll buy enough to fill the bathtub, my lady, for just one pretty smile."

She pasted on a smile and said, "Let's talk business, as in why you aren't working for Red."

"First you tell me about Conrad Oil Enterprises again. There's not an oil well anywhere near that lonesome old pumper on your property." He tipped the glass of iced tea back and guzzled more than half of it before coming up for air.

"Everyone thought I was crazy as old Cletus." She

laughed. "Remember him? He used to walk up and down the streets in Tishomingo, and he wore at least five watches on each wrist and blue plaid shorts."

"And a yellow checked sports coat and a big, wide tie with purple polka dots," he finished for her. "Gee, I hadn't thought about him in years. Remember how he used to hang around in front of the Armstrong Clothing Store? One day I asked him why he just stood there doing nothing, and he told me it was so everyone in town could see him. I didn't even crack a smile. I just nodded and went on."

"Everyone thought I was crazy to sink a well on this land." Her eyes sparkled in the candlelight. "Allie was ready to throw me out in front of a semi on a four-lane highway, and she was my best friend. She said that I could dig to China with a teaspoon and not find a tablespoon of corn oil, let alone crude. But I followed my hunch and it paid off. The president of the bank in Denison told me the only reason he was loaning me the money was because he'd always wanted a little place in the country, and when the bank foreclosed on my mortgage, he was buying it."

"Good Lord!" Clancy exclaimed. "You sure had a lot of adversity."

"Yep." She nodded.

The waiter brought their food and refilled their glasses, then disappeared again as Angel continued. "I was fresh out of college and no one offered me a job, so I took my savings and hired a driller. That's how I started Conrad Oil. I could've gone to work for Red and Anna after that. Red said he'd pay big bucks for me to sit behind a desk and tell him when I had a hunch, but I wanted more than that. I wanted a business so all my friends could work together. I worked hard, and now I've got my dream. The next year we incorporated Conrad Oil Enterprises. I hold the majority stake in the company and the girls all own shares too," she said between bites. "This is good food. I told you I was hungry. I can eat like a field hand, and I'm not one bit bashful about it," she added.

"Good." He nodded. "I like a woman who isn't afraid to chow down."

"What about you? Are you happy teaching? Funny, I always thought you'd go into the oil business somehow. When we talked, you were going to be an engineer, or a geologist just like I wanted to be."

"Red's been after me for a while to work for him. Says I shouldn't waste my science degree. I thought about it, but I don't know. Teaching is fun. I like the kids and I like having summers off so I can fool around." He winked at her. "I don't have to depend on a salary for my major income, thanks to the investments my dad left me. Do you want me to go to work for your competition?" he asked.

"Do whatever you want to do," she said. "Right now, I just want you to finish eating so we can play golf and drink wine," she told him.

It was after eleven when they finished the second round of golf. True to her word, Angel won the first round. Clancy barely came out the victor of the second game, and he prided himself on both his miniature and golf games. His ex-wife, Melissa, had hated both. She had never wanted to learn any game that took her outside where it was hot—where she might chip a nail or break a sweat.

But comparing Melissa and Angel wasn't fair to either of them. They were as different as two women could be. His mama called that kind of thing measuring one person by another's half bushel. He glanced over at Angel. She was smiling, so she was evidently pleased with her win, but she didn't say a word the rest of the way back to the motel.

Clancy parked the rental car in the spot marked with his room number, reached over the seat, and picked up a brown bag.

Angela smiled when she heard the tinkle of crystal glasses. She'd whipped him at golf, and if he was still as poor at drinking as he used to be, she might whip him at drinking too.

"Wine on the beach," he said when he opened the door for her. "Two glasses, one bottle. Half a glass and I'll be snoring, so there will be plenty for you." He took her hand and led her across the road to the sand.

He sat down and pulled her down beside him, then let go of her hand to take off his shoes and socks. He rolled up his khaki trousers haphazardly until they could go no further, just below his muscular thighs. "Got another one of those white thingy jigs?" He tapped the plastic ring that held one side of her dress high. "Tie up the other side and take off those shoes, and we'll go wading before we have a toast to the moonless night."

"I'm not afraid of getting my dress wet," Angel said.

"Oh, yeah?" Clancy scooped her up in his arms as if she weighed nothing and waded out into the ocean. "How much is it worth to you to keep it dry?" He pretended to almost let go of her.

"Clancy Morgan, if you drop me, I swear you're going to get wet too. Don't forget that summer at the dam," she taunted.

"How could I forget that summer?" He kissed her on the neck.

"Oh—" She pushed his face away and flipped out of his arms. Just as she hit the water, she grabbed both of his legs and brought him down beside her, dousing both of them.

"You are one bad, bad lady," he blubbered when he surfaced in the knee-deep water.

"Don't threaten me if you don't want to get wet." She backed up until she was sitting in water so shallow that she could feel the sand shifting under them every time the waves swelled in and ebbed back out. "I'm a grown woman now, Clancy, and you might not like me when you get to know me this time. Do you just feel guilty about our baby? You never knew him, not even for the nine months he was mine. I don't want you to feel like you've got to pay for your mistakes. You can't change the past and neither can I. And like you said, you thought I would probably give him away." Angel had come to grips with that much. Maybe she and Clancy could be friends.

He reached across the wet sand to touch her hand. "I know that. But right now, I'm trying to deal with feelings I didn't even really know I had. Ten years ago, my hormones ruled my brain, and I was young and just plain stupid. Now,

I hope I'm a little smarter. I want to get to know you again, Angel. And I'd want to know you even if we hadn't been together back then."

"Thanks." She looked him in the eye, reassured that he wasn't shooting her some practiced line.

"I believe we have wine to celebrate our first evening together again." He lay back on the sandbar, reached as far back as he could, and grabbed the sack. "And wineglasses." He pulled out two cut-crystal, stemmed glasses wrapped in white linen napkins. "One bottle of rare, vintage Asti from the vineyards of Italy, personally stomped just for us by purple-footed peasants."

She giggled and a thousand stars lit up in Clancy's soul. It didn't matter if there were dark clouds hanging low in the sky, or that he didn't know a thing about Italian vineyards; he could have just listened to her laughter all night. Maybe he'd send all her friends at Conrad Oil bouquets of roses tomorrow morning, just for giving him the chance to be near Angel again.

"To new beginnings." Clancy poured for both of them, handed her a wineglass by its slender stem, and clinked his glass to hers. He downed the mouthful of sparkling wine in one gulp.

She swished the wine around until its fragrance wafted up to her nose, then sipped it delicately. "Mmm," she said. "I intend to enjoy every single little bubble, not send it down my throat like a shot."

"Well, that's the only way I can get it down. I still don't really like wine, or beer, or bourbon. I've never acquired a taste for any of it," he admitted.

She tasted the sparkling wine again. "Suit yourself. But I think a glass of white wine on a sandbar on a moonless night is pure heaven."

Warm seawater sloshed up to her hips, billowing the skirt of her dress, and then the wave receded, leaving ripples in the sand on which they sat. Clancy watched the tiny sand crabs pop up and try to bury themselves again in the soft, wet muck before the next splash washed over them.

Oh, to be able to sit forever in such peacefulness, he thought. No meddling friends, no interference. Just blissful solitude as he watched her sip from the crystal wineglass he'd provided.

"Are you going back to Oklahoma City to teach, or will you resign and work for Red since he's moving his operation back to Texas?" She held the wineglass up to the faint light from the motel behind the dune. "You said he offered you a job, but you didn't ever say if you would even consider it."

"I don't know. But I can't keep Red dangling and feel right about it. I asked my mom for advice. She said to follow my heart just the way she's following hers and let the rest of the world be damned," he answered.

"Oh? What did Meredith mean by that?" Angel finished her wine and gently placed the crystal glass in the sand.

"My mother and Tom Lloyd are getting married today in San Antonio. They wanted it to be just the two of them for the wedding, but they plan on celebrating in style when we get back," Clancy answered.

"Tom Lloyd? You mean the—" Her eyes grew wide. "Isn't he the supervisor at the cemetery?"

"Yep, Tom Lloyd, and yes, he still takes care of the cemetery. Seems she met him while she was out there tending to Dad's grave, and they got to talking. He lost his wife a while back and he was lonely too," Clancy explained.

"But—" Angel cocked her head to one side. "Meredith has always been so..."

"I know." Clancy nodded. "Shocked me too. Know what she told me? She said she didn't need money, and she didn't care what her friends thought of him. Tom makes her feel special, and Mama says everyone can get used to it or they can go to hell."

Angel sighed. "Well, I'll be damned."

He laughed. "You know, I thought she'd die a thousand times if I ever told her about you and the baby. Guess I was wrong about that too! She's as disappointed in what I did as I am, and I felt like a teenager getting in trouble when I told her."

"Tom Lloyd's wife was my granny's friend. Sometimes she even helped clean houses when Granny got behind. I always thought that Tom was the tallest man in the whole world when I was a little girl, and the last time I saw him, he *still* seemed like a kindly giant. He never raised his voice. But he is still only the maintenance supervisor at the cemetery—and Clancy, your mother is probably one of the richest women in all of Johnston County!"

"I reckon there'll be talk in Tishomingo," he said. "But neither of us cares about that."

"Yep, I imagine there will be." Angel lay back on the sandbar to look up at the sky.

"Hello, Clancy," a familiar voice said.

"Melissa. What are you doing here?" He jerked his head around.

"Who's your little friend?" Melissa said sarcastically.

Angel didn't turn around. *Of all the times for Clancy's ex to show up*, she thought bitterly.

"I said, what in the hell are you doing here?" Clancy asked again with a cutting edginess in his voice.

"Don't use profanity with me," Melissa replied prissily.

How on earth had she even known where he was? In less than a month, she'd shown up on two sandbars just to torment him. "Folks back home said you'd come down here for a little vacation, and I just thought you might like some company. I had a hunch that you'd come down here to drink in secret. If your little habit is getting out of control, I'd really like to help you. It breaks my heart to know that I can still make you so unhappy after all these years." She fidgeted with the silver bracelets on her wrist, sliding them up and down with a clatter that annoyed Angel no end.

Melissa sighed loudly. "But I see you've picked up a bottle to drown your sorrows and talked a beach bunny into joining you. Aren't you going to introduce me?"

"Why?" Angel stood up, her soggy dress clinging to every curve of her body. "He shouldn't have to introduce us, Melissa. After all, you and I were in school together for thirteen years. I remember you very well. But maybe you don't remember me. I'm Angela Conrad."

Chapter 10

"Of course I remember you." Melissa's tone turned to ice. "He told me that you blamed him for getting you pregnant. Everyone knows he wouldn't have anything to do with you."

"I loved him when all you saw was a handsome groom to stand beside you at your picture-perfect little wedding," Angela told her.

"Melissa, what are you doing here? If you're stalking me, I'm asking you to stop and forget all about me." Clancy slowly got to his feet.

"Of course you didn't ask me to come down here, darling." Melissa turned away from Angel as if she were beneath consideration. "But I figured you should be the first one to know some very special news. Our news will change your mind about things."

"Don't tell me you flew all the way down here to tell me you're getting a divorce from Daniel. The scuttlebutt around Tishomingo has already let that news out into the public," Clancy said disbelievingly. "I remember when you divorced me for him, and I didn't care anymore by that point. What makes you think I'd care now?"

"Oh, hush." Melissa took a step forward and put her palms on his chest. "Did you know that Tishomingo is buzzing right now about your mother? My mama is horrified that Meredith Morgan is off somewhere in Texas marrying old Tom Lloyd. Your dear daddy's only been gone four years and she's taken up with a man like that, but I'm not here to pass judgment on Meredith." Melissa's smirky tone of voice hadn't changed.

"Then why are you here? State your business and then please, please, go away and leave me alone," Clancy said. "How did you even find me here?"

Angel watched the scene between them, transfixed, as if it were from one of those soap operas her granny had felt compelled to watch every day of the week.

Melissa stuck out her lower lip in a childish pout. "Oh, all right. Meredith has my friend Christy house-sitting for her while she and Tom are off on their *honeymoon*." She dragged out the last word as if she were a kid with a new dirty term that she was showing off in front of the whole playground. "Christy found a note that had the name of your motel and the phone number here in case of an emergency, and she told my mama. And I caught the next flight out, right behind you, to tell you the wonderful news I just mentioned."

"I don't give a damn if you bought me the winning ticket in the Texas lottery. You can have the zillion-dollar jackpot all to yourself. Just so long as you leave me alone." Clancy picked up the bottle of Asti and the two wineglasses. "You can just trot back to the airport and catch the next flight home. Come on, Angel. I'll walk you to your door."

Melissa took a step back and stomped her foot in the sand, practically falling off her high-heeled sandal when she did it. She put her hands on her waist and glared at him, as if a look could change the way he felt about her.

Angel glared at her. Damn the woman for having the nerve to follow Clancy down here!

"See you later, Melissa," she said hatefully. "You, too, Clancy. I don't need a love triangle in my life." She picked up her sandals and started to walk away.

"Don't go," he said just above a whisper. "Please, don't go."

"Why not?" Melissa turned and lifted her shoulders like an offended female feline. "She might be rich now, but she'll always be white trash."

"Shut up, Melissa!" Clancy said furiously. "Don't you know it's over for us? Has been for years. Whether Angela stays or goes is her business, but nothing you can say would make me love *you* again…if I ever did."

Angel doubled up her fists, but she kept them down and fought the white-hot rage boiling up inside her. One good solid right hook and this useless woman would be sporting a crooked nose until she could see a plastic surgeon. But she fought back the urge to sock Melissa hard enough to send her about halfway to the horizon.

"You *will* love me when I tell you our good news," she smiled.

Angel fumed silently.

"I know you wanted to have a child when we were married, and things just never seemed to work out. I'm real sorry about that. I'm pregnant, Clancy. And the baby is yours." Melissa's tone was unbearably smug, and her expression seemed to dare either of her listeners to doubt her announcement.

"You're *what*?" Clancy asked incredulously.

"You heard me. Preg. Nant. *Pregnant*. Only by a couple

of weeks, but you know how good these early tests are now. Must have happened that night at Pennington Creek when you were so drunk you didn't know what you were doing. Don't you remember any of it, darling?" Melissa shot a fake smile toward Angel.

That funny feeling Angel called "the hunch" came over her. It started down deep where the anger had come from just moments before.

She mentally picked up the pieces of this particular puzzle and put them together. Her intuition had never yet disappointed her. Angela had founded a multimillion-dollar business based on it—and she'd be a fool to let this brazen bitch control her emotions or her life when she suddenly felt a hunch as strongly as she did right then.

"You might be pregnant"—Clancy shook his head in bewilderment—"but it's not mine and you know it. Nothing happened, except that you slapped me when I told you about the stillborn baby Angela had. That baby was mine. I might have had a few beers when you showed up again, but I remember when I've had sex, and I didn't."

"You were so drunk you wouldn't remember anything," Melissa smoothed the front of her skirt over her flat stomach. "You offered me bourbon, and then you called me Angel.

Then I sat down on the sand beside you, and that's when you started kissing me, and one thing led to another."

Angela stifled a laugh. This would make Granny's soap operas as tame as a declawed house kitten. Melissa was lying, and Angela knew it as surely as she knew Clancy was telling the truth. So, Melissa needed a husband. That meant the baby wasn't Daniel's or she would still be with him. This would definitely set the old Tishomingo tongues to wagging! The social cream of the crop had gotten caught with her lacy underbritches down around her ankles.

"What are you laughing at, Angela? You had your turn to have a baby with him. Now it's mine," Melissa sneered.

"Don't take that tone with me, Melissa. I'm not beneath you and I'm not the shy kid in the classroom you used to pick on. I'm a grown woman who's smart enough to know when another woman is making a fool of herself. If you're pregnant, congratulations. When the baby's born, Clancy can go to the hospital for DNA testing." Angel moved over next to him and slipped her arm through his. "If it's Clancy's baby, then he'll be more than happy to write you a support check, but you and I both know that the baby isn't his. Get back in your car, wherever it is, and get the hell out of here. Because this beach ain't big enough for us both, and I'm staying."

Clancy didn't know whether to spit or go blind. He expected Angel to walk away from him and never look back, and he wouldn't have blamed her if she did. What in the world had happened in the middle of this argument to change her mind? Here she was plastered to his wet side as if she belonged there, and Melissa just stood in front of them with her mouth hanging open.

"Just remember, if I couldn't keep him, you don't have a chance," Melissa said. "He's never been faithful and never will be. I'm the only person in the whole world who ever understood him."

"Honey, you couldn't keep him because I had him first." Angel couldn't resist the barb. "Clancy, I do believe you said something about walking me to my door. Maybe you'd like to come in for a soda while I have another glass of this wonderful wine. I heard there was a storm rolling in tonight, Melissa. I hope you don't have trouble on your return flight. Come on, Clancy. These wet clothes are beginning to get sandy and I need a shower." She pulled him away.

"Clancy, if you walk away with that bitch, you'll never see this baby." Melissa raised her voice, and Angel's flat-palmed slap answered her.

"Don't call me names," Angel ground out. "Clancy won't have to see this baby of yours, because when the tests come back, it won't be his. I'd be willing to stake Conrad Oil on it, Melissa, and you know I'm right, so go find some other sucker to pin your mistake on."

"Are you going to let Angel run your life and treat me, the mother of your child, like this?" Melissa held her red cheek and let a few well-trained tears run down to her quivering jawbone.

"She can run my life like a toy train." Clancy smiled.

"Then both of you can go straight to hell, and, Clancy, you can just wonder until this child is born if this baby belongs to you." Melissa stomped silently through the sand and back to her car, where she slammed the door and peeled out.

Angel sat right back down in the water and poured herself another glass of wine. "And now, what have you got to say for yourself?"

Clancy's heart fell again. She would never believe that he had told the truth. She'd certainly never trust him again, and they hadn't even begun to renew their romance. In fact, they were back where they started, and he was sure he'd never see the day when he'd take her to dinner again.

"This is what happened. I left you at the cemetery, stopped

by the liquor store, got some beer and bourbon, and decided I'd get drunk and give myself a hellacious headache. I wanted to hurt so much that I couldn't think of you and I wouldn't see that tombstone with my son's name on it. I wanted to forget what a jerk I'd been to you, and a good old-fashioned hangover seemed like an appropriate punishment." Clancy sat down beside her.

The pieces were tumbling into place in her hunch factory again. Clancy was telling the truth. "I see. And where did you go to create this humongous headache?"

"To the dam," Clancy answered. "I took an old blanket and spread it out in our spot, and I sat down on the sandbar and put my feet in the water and started drinking beers. One minute I was all by myself. The next minute, Melissa was there beside me. At first, I thought it was you. I guess I hoped it was you. Melissa thought she'd ruined my life by divorcing me, so I told her the truth about why I was getting drunk. She slapped my face and stormed off, saying if I didn't tell my mother the whole story, she would the next day."

"And did you?" Angel held her breath.

"Yep, I did," he answered. "I thought she was going to take a hickory switch to me even though I'm twenty-eight years old and survived a marriage to that witch and then the divorce. Then she told me about Tom, and I told her I realized what a big mistake I made all those years ago."

"Then your mother knows about me?" Angel whispered.

He nodded. "When I told her about your friends giving you this vacation, she said it was good that I was flying down here. She said that to face the future, I had to bury the past and learn to appreciate the present, or some philosophical thing like that. Seemed smart to me at the time. I sure never expected to look up and see Melissa on the beach tonight. Whatever possessed her to fly down here is a mystery to me, Angel. That baby is not mine, I promise."

Angel thought for a long moment. "It's all pretty plain to me. She and her husband, Daniel, are getting a divorce. Being alone and pregnant is scary, Clancy. She moved out of her parents' house into the dorms and a secure relationship with you, then into marriage with you, and then into marriage with him as soon as possible. The divorce isn't final, and she's losing her security blanket. She doesn't care if her old blanket is a bit worn around the edges and tattered, it's better than nothing."

"Are you saying I'm nothing?" Clancy asked.

"I'm explaining her actions," Angela answered. "Melissa's scared to face life alone. At one time, she could control you, and it might have worked again if I hadn't been there beside you. Her story didn't make sense. You won't even have a full glass of wine with me, but you'd get drunk with the woman who left you for another man? Come on, even you have a bit more class than that."

"Thanks, and I do mean it." He sighed. "I really did not have sex with her. I had drunk several beers and I was a little tipsy, but I did not touch her, and that's a promise. If she's pregnant, I'll go for DNA testing, I promise."

"That's up to you, but it would be a smart thing to do if she insists on spreading rumors about you," Angela said. "For now, I think I'd like to call it a day. I need a long, hot shower to wash all this sand out of my underwear, and you, sir, probably do too. You can walk me to my door. But I was only kidding about you coming into my room for a cold soda. I learned my lesson about sex many years ago. I don't fall into bed with a man just because he has lots of sex appeal and a nice smile."

"Thanks for the compliments." Clancy extended a hand to help her up.

They walked across the sandbar still holding hands. Angel had no doubt that the head of all the guardian angels in heaven had been working on her side that night. She felt a crazy need to drop down on her knees and give thanks even if she never knew exactly what had caused her to turn around in the middle of that triangular argument.

Thank God for hunches, she thought.

Angel hadn't realized how much Clancy meant to her until she thought of Melissa snaring him with a lie. She might not be ready for a relationship with him, but she'd be damned if she stood by and lost the best golfing partner she'd ever found. And, besides, she got the whole bottle of wine when they were celebrating!

When they reached the top of the stairs, he unlocked her door for her, handed back the key, and turned around to go across the breezeway to the second building. "Thanks. I mean it, Angel."

"Is that all? I didn't say I wouldn't appreciate a nice warm kiss to finish off a wonderful day." Angel smiled up at him.

He wrapped his arms around her and drew her close to his body. He cupped her cheeks in his hands, and she'd barely had time to moisten her lips when his eyes fluttered shut and his mouth closed over hers. Her knees turned to jelly, and she leaned in to him for support.

"Is that warm enough?" he whispered seductively when the kiss ended.

She took a step back and said, "No, that wasn't warm. It was downright hot! I'll see you tomorrow."

"I'll bring the doughnuts for breakfast if you'll make a pot of coffee," he said. "About nine?"

"Make it ten," she answered. "We are on vacation."

"Yes, ma'am." He grinned.

She opened her door, stepped inside, and kicked off her shoes as she crossed the room and fell onto the bed. When she touched her lips, she was surprised to find that they were cool. She could have sworn that they would be burning like fire.

Chapter 11

SHE LAY THERE FOR SEVERAL MINUTES, THEN GOT UP AND took a long, cool shower. She crawled between the crisp, white sheets and stared at the ceiling for a minute or two before she drifted off to a dream about Clancy. When the alarm went off, it jolted her out of a deep sleep. She slapped at the clock to turn it off, but it rang again and she realized that it was the telephone.

She glanced at the time and realized it was only four o'clock in the morning. "Damn it, Clancy." She grabbed the phone from the nightstand and closed her eyes before she answered.

"Hello. This had better be a matter of life and death," she said.

"Miss Conrad, this is the front desk. We're sorry to inform

you that you'll have to leave within the next hour. We are evacuating the motel, and the whole area for that matter. The tropical storm has made a turnaround and will be making landfall by tomorrow afternoon as a hurricane. We don't usually get this type of storm during this time of year. We're going to be boarding up windows and doors all day. Can I assist you in any way?"

"Good grief!" Angel jumped out of bed and onto her feet.

"We've been tracking her path all night. The Weather Channel had predicted she'd go to the other side of the state, but she made an abrupt about-face and is coming this way with a full head of steam."

"Thank you," Angel managed to say before she hung up and threw a suitcase on the bed. She tossed clothing in it and rushed to the bathroom for her toiletries. Then she made herself calm down and fished her phone out of her purse, found the number of the airline, and called. "I need a flight out of here to Dallas or Oklahoma City."

"Sorry, ma'am. The flights that haven't been canceled are already full," the reservations clerk said, and Angela swore under her breath at the same time she heard an incessant pounding on her door. She jerked it open to find Clancy standing outside with his bags sitting beside him.

"I've called the car rental where I got the Cadillac. My truck is at the Oklahoma City airport. We can leave this rental there and drive my truck back to Tishomingo, or I'll take you home. Get in touch with your rental place and tell them to pick up your car here at the hotel." He pushed past her, zipped her two suitcases, and started out the door with them.

"Wait a minute!" she called desperately. "What if I don't want to ride all the way home with you?"

He groaned and threw up his palms. "You can go with me, drive yourself, or we can ride out the storm on the beach. The motel is evacuating. I'll be back in two minutes, Angela. You don't have to get dressed. You look pretty cute in that nightshirt, and I'll drive, so you can sleep."

"Oh, hush!" She slammed the door, shucked her Betty Boop nightshirt and threw on the shorts and T-shirt she had left out to wear home, then dialed the rental company number on the key chain she'd pitched on the night table yesterday.

Was it really just yesterday that she had arrived at the hotel? A whole month's worth of staggering events had happened in a scant twenty-four hours, and now a freak tropical storm had decided to pay a visit. Did she have her girlfriends to thank for that too? She tapped her fingers on the table and willed someone to answer the phone.

Maybe the rental agency had been evacuated too!

"Thank you for calling Hertz," the rental clerk said. "How can I help you?"

Was Florida full of crazy people who had no respect for storms? And what did they do with tourists who needed a place to stay when the beach motels were evacuated?

"This is Angela Conrad. I need to return a rental," she said. "Could you please pick it up here at the hotel?"

"We're here twenty-four hours a day," the clerk said. "Leave the keys under the vehicle's floor mat. We'll bring a set of keys and drive it home. Angela Conrad, red Ford Taurus. Do you want us to credit the refund back to your credit card? Do you need the address of a shelter where you can stay for the next couple of days until the hurricane blows over?"

"Thank you. And, yes, please do credit it back to my card." Angela hopped on one foot while she put on a sneaker.

"Better hurry if you're planning on making a run for the border," the woman said. "Most hotels north of us will be filling up fast. Be careful of floodwaters over streets."

"Will do." Angela crammed everything from the vanity in the bathroom in her last bag, quickly scanned the room, and was on the landing by the time Clancy came back up.

They were thirty minutes inland, headed due north, when the wind and rain surrounded the car on all sides. Clancy eased up on the gas pedal and inched along the highway behind dozens of other people trying to get away from the hurricane. He gripped the steering wheel so tightly that his knuckles were white. Angel had never seen such rain in her life. Visibility was two inches at most. Wind beat the powerful, driving sheet of water against the car in great waves.

"Maybe we should've built an ark last night," Angel whispered, awed by the force of the storm. "If this is just the forerunner of the hurricane, I don't want to be around when the real storm arrives."

"Maybe we should have found a shelter and not tried to outrun this," Clancy said. "The hotel manager said the hurricane wouldn't actually make landfall until tomorrow."

"Shh," she yelled above the noise of the wind. "I don't want to spend time in a shelter full of strangers. We'll outrun the storm soon enough. Too bad we can't take part of this rain home, only without the wind. You know how much my gardener would like this amount of water in the middle of

July?" she said nervously as she watched a tree on the side of the road bend and sway, then disappear in the grayness.

They could easily die in this stupid Cadillac out here in the middle of gray rain, and no one would know for days. When rescue workers came to clean up the rubble, there would be an overturned car, looking like a casket, with two bodies in it. What in the hell would the Tishomingo newspaper do with that story? Angel could just imagine the lead: *Well-known local resident dies in crash with rich oil company president, formerly a local member of the white-trash sector, and his former wife says she barely got out of the state before the storm hit!*

I bet the wrath of Melissa caused the hurricane to take an abrupt turn toward us, Angel thought. After all, the woman had been a first-class witch for years. Maybe she had taken a correspondence course and expanded her powers. Angel visualized her in a long, flowing black robe, stirring a boiling pot full of liquid somewhere down the beach. In the vision, Melissa would chant a while and then add a pile of frog toes and the powdered brain cells of a sea gull, along with a sprinkle of lizard liver, evoking the dark powers to bury Clancy and Angel together in a big automobile.

Angel giggled softly at the crazy notion, but hey, it had kept her from worrying for a few minutes.

By what should have been daylight, they had crossed the state line into Alabama and had only traveled sixty miles in three hours. The rain slacked up enough to make it possible to see the road signs and the yellow line down the middle of the highway. Angel's stomach grumbled loudly enough that Clancy turned to look at her.

"Hungry?" he asked. "I'm starving. Want to stop at the next exit? I caught a glimpse of an advertisement a few miles back that said there was a McDonald's up ahead. I'd do anything for a cup of coffee."

Angel sighed. "Yes. I want mine black and strong. And one of those biscuits with eggs and ham and cheese, and a hash brown. Do you think it's going to rain on us all the way home?"

Clancy nodded. "Probably." He eased the car off the exit ramp, noticed a McDonald's sign to the left, and after a quarter of a mile saw the familiar arches. "We're going to get soaked." He parked the car, turned off the engine, and just sat there.

"Are you all right?" Angel asked.

"My hands hurt from gripping this steering wheel so hard, and my shoulders feel like someone beat me," he admitted.

She reached across the console and patted him on the

back. "Thank you for getting us out of there. I'm strong, but I'm sure glad I didn't have to drive in all this rain."

"You are welcome. Do you want to go to the drive-through window and eat in the car?" he asked.

She unbuckled her seat belt. "I'm going in. I've got to go to the restroom. Better to be wet with rainwater than with what would happen if I don't find the ladies' room. Besides, I'm not sugar or salt, and I won't melt. All that will happen is my curly hair will frizz up and I'll look like a string mop left out in the sun."

"Then let's make a run for it. Betcha I can beat you," he teased.

"Oh yeah?" She took the challenge. "On your mark, open the door, go!" Angel splashed through the water, ignored all the mud puddles, and laughed all the way. When Clancy reached the door, she was holding it open for him like a butler. "Come right in, Clancy Morgan. You just lost the race. So, you can buy breakfast. Besides, I left my purse in the car. I'll be sitting at that booth after I dry off with paper towels in the restroom." She pointed to the back and left him standing in a puddle.

"Yes, ma'am." He grinned.

When she returned, he motioned to her from a booth where their breakfast was sitting in the middle of the table.

Her shirt clung to every curve, and there wasn't a dry patch of cloth on her body. She took off her shoes and set them on the seat beside her.

"Breakfast is served, ma'am." Clancy pointed at the tray between them. "Chow down. The lady at the register said it's a hundred miles to Montgomery and there's not a dry inch of ground between here and there. We might make it by lunchtime if we're lucky."

"Umm." She tasted the coffee first, holding it in her mouth, enjoying the warmth and the flavor. "Thanks for this. Want me to drive a while? How far is it by car to Dallas from Alabama, anyway?"

"Depends on where you start from, but we've got two weeks to get there, don't we?" he said.

"No." She bit into the biscuit. "I might keep company with you for two weeks in a resort, but not in a car. We can drive straight through until we get there. You can sleep while I drive, and I'll sleep while you drive. A day, two days?"

"Two if the rain stops. One night in a motel on the way," he answered. "You're off work for two weeks, though. Let's take our time."

"I'm goin' home, Clancy," Angel declared as if that would make it final. "You can drop me in Denison on your way."

"Is your car at the airport?" he asked.

"Patty drove me to DFW," she said between bites. "I should call her. She'll think we both got blown away by this storm."

"When we drop this car off at the airport and get my truck, I'd love it if you'd come home with me for the rest of the vacation. Mama would love to see you," he asked.

Angel practically choked on the hash-brown patty. "Are you seriously inviting me to go home with you? To Tishomingo—as a house guest in your mother's home?"

"Yes, I am." He nodded. "Or I'll get you a room at the only motel in town for the rest of your vacation if you'd be more comfortable there. Better yet, we've got a guesthouse out by the pool. It's got two separate rooms with two outside entrances. You can stay in one, and I'll stay in the other. That way Mom and Tom can have a little bit of privacy in the house. It is their honeymoon, remember?"

"Can I think about it for a while?" Angel wasn't going to make a big decision like that on the spur of the moment.

"Sure. I figure we might get in by tomorrow evening if the rain lets up," he said.

Angel called Patty about the time that the office opened. She got voicemail and left a message telling her friend that she was in a world of trouble, that the storm hadn't blown her and Clancy away, and she'd call again in a couple of days. Then she ran back to the car in the driving rain and hopped into the backseat. By the time Clancy opened the door to his side of the car, she was opening a suitcase, taking out clean underwear, a dry shirt, and pair of shorts, and jerking her wet shirt over her head.

"Keep your eyes on the front window," she told him when he dove for the front seat. "I'm changing clothes back here, and then I'm crawling over the seat. You can do the same when I'm finished. Unless you're too damned tall and old to crawl over the seat. Lord, it feels wonderful to wear dry clothes. I'm glad I brought these old sweatpants and this shirt. They're soft and warm. I may sleep all the way to Oklahoma City in them."

"Why do I have to keep my eyes front and center? There are windows all around you in this vehicle," he reminded her. "Anyone can see inside."

She dried her hair with a beach towel and then threw it over the seat. "Want to use this to get the water out of your hair? Anyone would have to press his nose to the window to see inside in all this rain. Then he'd break his neck to cop a peek because I can dress faster than the speed of lightning."

She wiggled into her dry things. "Now"—she shimmied over the seat—"your turn."

"You don't have to keep your eyes on the front." Clancy opened the door and quickly went from the front to the backseat where he opened his suitcase. "I don't mind one bit if you turn around and stare at me."

"I'll just look forward," she declared, but she didn't tell him she could see him from the chest up in the corner of the rearview mirror.

He finished dressing, then crawled over the seat with as much agility as she had. "I haven't been wet like that—"

"Since early last night, but it didn't feel the same then, did it?" She finished the sentence for him. "That was voluntary."

She curled up in the seat, leaned her head against the window, and fell asleep by the time he had started the car and pulled out into the traffic. When she awoke, she rubbed her eyes and yawned. "What time is it?"

"After two," he answered.

"Look!" She pointed out his window, just missing his nose by an inch in her excitement to show him. "That's the most beautiful rainbow I've ever seen. The colors are so bright. Look at that purple, Clancy!"

"I can see it, Angel, honest. Want me to stop the car so it won't get away before you've looked your fill?" he asked.

"Look at the blue. And I can see the whole arch. Do you think there's a pot of gold at the bottom?" She was so excited that her words came out in a tumble.

"You're the one with the hunch power, Angel. What do you think is at the bottom of the arch? A pot of gold or an oil well?" he asked.

"A motel with hot water and big, fluffy towels," she answered.

"Your wish is my command," he said as he pulled under the awning of the Holiday Inn. "One room or two?" he asked before he got out of the car.

Her heart screamed one, but her mind knew better. "It doesn't matter. One if it's got two beds. Two if they've only got a bed in each. I'm not afraid of you, Clancy, but we're sleeping in separate beds tonight, and that's a fact." She crawled out of the car and headed into the motel lobby with him.

"Whatever you want," he told her.

"We need a couple of rooms," Clancy said.

"Got one left," the clerk said. "And it's close to the restaurant and club too. They serve a pretty mean surf-and-turf supper there, and a band plays on Friday and Saturday, but not tonight."

"We'll take it," Angel said.

The clerk filled in all the paperwork, took Clancy's ID and credit card, then handed him a door key.

"We can have dinner without going outside." Clancy got a cart for their luggage and loaded it up. "But I guess there'll be no dancing, since it's only Thursday night. However, if you'd like to stay over through tomorrow night, we can rest up all day, and I'll dance the soles right off your shoes."

"Oh sure, and take until Saturday night to get to Tishomingo." She shook her head. "No, thank you! Cooling my heels in a motel is not exactly what I had in mind for a vacation after all these years. But then a danged old hurricane, a twenty-four-hour drive, and kinky hair wasn't either. Show me to the room and let me have a shower before I turn into a raving lunatic."

"Then you are coming to Tishomingo with me?" Clancy asked as he pushed the cart into the elevator and pushed the button to the third floor.

"I think I just might do that," she said as the elevator doors opened. "I figure in less than a week, you'll be glad to give me a ride back to Denison. You might even get a bottle of wine to celebrate your good fortune in getting rid of me!"

He tapped the room key against the lock and opened the door.

Angel went into the room and pointed to the bed farthest from the door and closest to the bathroom. "I'd like to have that bed, and can I have the first shower?"

"Of course." He smiled. "Go enjoy a nice long shower or bath. I'll take a nap while you do that."

"I'd love a nap after my shower," Angel said.

"I'll wake you at suppertime." He yawned as he unloaded the cart and then pushed it out into the hallway.

Angel unzipped one of her cases, took out her toiletry kit and a white terry bathrobe, and disappeared into the bathroom.

She ran a tub of full of hot water and dropped her clothing on the floor. She sighed when she stepped into the tub and slid down into the warm water. Poor Clancy must be even more sore and tired than she was. She had slept through part of the trip, but he had driven for hours and hours. When the water went lukewarm, she washed her hair and got out of the tub. She wrapped a white hotel towel around her hair, dried her body off, and then slipped into her white terry robe.

"Good grief!" she exclaimed when she saw her reflection in the vanity mirror and realized what she had agreed to do. "I've agreed to spend time with him in Tishomingo. What was I thinking?"

Clancy was too tense to fall asleep when he lay down. His mind went over and over what had happened in the past twenty-four hours. He had been sure Angel would walk away from him last night at the beach when Melissa announced she was pregnant. Then he figured she'd throw a fit at even the mention of spending the rest of her long-deferred vacation in Tishomingo. Their hometown was so small there wasn't anything to do but a little golfing and fishing, unless Blake Shelton had country artists coming to town for a show. Still, the thought of going there seemed to brighten her eyes and perk her up more than anything he'd mentioned since the alumni reunion. Then it dawned on him why it was so important to her. He would be taking her around town like a girlfriend—like he should have done years ago.

Chapter 12

Wearing nothing but a robe and a towel around her head, Angel slipped out into the hotel room to find Clancy sleeping. She quietly opened her suitcase, found a pair of pajama pants and an oversize T-shirt and went back to the bathroom to get dressed. When she came out the second time, she pulled back the covers in the second bed and bit back a moan of pure pleasure when she crawled between the sheets.

She rolled over and propped up on an elbow so she could stare her fill of Clancy. Even in sleep he looked tired. His dark beard put a shadow on his face, and his thick lashes fanned out over his chiseled cheeks. He'd been a handsome teenager, but he had grown into a sexy man—and she still felt the same about him as she did when they were younger.

Finally, her eyes grew heavy and she lay down, still facing him, and stared at him until she fell asleep. Darkness had filled the room when she awoke a few hours later. The bed next to Angel was empty, but she could hear water running in the bathroom shower. She groaned when she realized she had drifted off with the towel around her head. Taming her wild, curly hair would take hours.

Clancy came out of the bathroom wearing a towel and a smile. "Good morning, or is it evening?"

A wave of the same cologne he wore back in high school wafted across the room toward her and set her senses to reeling. He picked out a pair of pajama bottoms and a shirt from his suitcase and started back to the bathroom.

"I believe it's evening, or maybe even midnight," she answered.

"I'm starving." Clancy poked his head out around the bathroom door. "What are you hungry for? Want to get something delivered to our room or go out?"

"Pizza in our room," she answered, thinking that she could just pile her hair up in a messy bun and not worry with straightening it and getting dressed.

Clancy dressed and then came back into the room, sat down at the desk located at the end of his bed, and picked up a hotel directory. He flipped through it, stopped on a full-page ad for a pizza place, and looked up at Angel. "What kind do you like?"

"Meat lover's with black olives," she answered.

And there you go! Susan's voice popped into her head. *He doesn't even know what kind of pizza you like, or ice cream either, for that matter, because he was too ashamed of you to take you out on a real date.*

Clancy ordered what she wanted and then ordered a Hawaiian pizza for himself, plus an order of breadsticks and extra marinara sauce.

See, I was right! Y'all don't even have the same taste in pizza. Patty continued to give her the con side of letting Clancy back into her life.

That's a minor detail, Angel argued. *The bunch of you sent me on this trip to get closure. I can do it without your help.*

Clancy finished the call by asking for an order of cinnamon sticks and a two-liter bottle of root beer before he laid the phone on the desk, rolled the chair around, and propped his feet on the end of his bed.

"Supper will arrive in twenty minutes," he said.

"Clancy, we can't go back in time." Angel propped two

pillows up on the head of the bed and rested her back against them.

"The last thing I want to do is go back in time," he drawled. "I wouldn't relive the past ten years for all the oil in Texas and half the tea in China. Not unless I could go back with the full knowledge I have today and redo most of it. I want to forget the past and enjoy the present, thanks to you"—Clancy caught her eye, and it seemed like he was looking right into her soul—"and have warm, fuzzy thoughts of the future. We've both got heartaches we need to get over. And I truly believe the place to do it is in Tishomingo. That's where it all started, so let's go back there and finish it, one way or the other."

"You're right," she agreed.

Angel wondered if it had just been a dream that she'd lolled in the calm waters in her sundress and drunk wine from a crystal goblet with Clancy. Maybe after a while someone would pinch her and she'd awaken in her bedroom at the farm and smell the aroma of bacon coming from the kitchen where Hilda rattled pots and pans, and Jimmy puttered around in the garden.

Clancy flipped his chair around and picked up the remote. "Want to watch a movie? We can pretend we're on a date."

Not until you take me to the Dairy Queen in Tishomingo, she thought.

"All right," she said as she watched him surf through the channels until he found the one that gave him the schedule for the evening. "*Something to Talk About* is coming on in ten minutes. It's a comedy with Julia Roberts," he said.

"I haven't had much time for movies," she said. "But I do like Julia Roberts."

"You could sit next to me for the movie." Clancy moved to his bed and propped up the pillows like she had done. "If we were on a real date at the movie theater in Tishomingo, you would be sitting next to me."

"Nope, this is fine." Angel readjusted her pillows and got comfortable. She couldn't remember the last time she'd watched a movie or had two whole hours to do nothing. If Conrad Oil Enterprises didn't claim her hours, then the farm did.

"Oh!" she exclaimed, remembering a promise she'd made to herself. "I've got to call Patty before the movie starts and tell her that the guillotine that's going to chop off her head is only held up by a skinny hair." She dialed the familiar number and got voicemail, which she talked to in a tone she hated but always used when talking to a silly machine.

"Patty, pick up the phone if you're there." She smiled when she thought again of the power of the tropical storm and her previous thoughts of Melissa doing a witchy version of the "Git Up" dance around a boiling cauldron. "We've survived another day and I'm going to Tishomingo for a while, but I'll be home soon. Remember, all of you...are... in...trouble," Angel singsonged.

"Movie time," Clancy announced.

Thank goodness the movie started with the credits, so they didn't miss anything when the delivery guy knocked on the hotel door. Clancy handed him some bills and set the boxes on the end of Angel's bed, then grabbed the ice bucket and hurried out into the hallway. In seconds, he was back and filled two plastic hotel cups with ice. He poured root beer into each of them and handed one to her.

"How do you want to do this?" he asked.

"You can sit beside me, and we'll have supper while we watch the movie." She took a sip of the root beer. "We're adults. We can sit on the same bed while we eat without..." She blushed and wasn't sure who she was trying to convince— him or herself.

Clancy tossed the pillows from his bed over to hers and made himself comfortable. He opened all the boxes and nodded toward her. "Dig in. I'll share my Hawaiian if I can have a slice of your meat lover's."

Aha, she thought. *We aren't as different as you thought, Miz Susan.*

They laughed all through the movie, and at one point, she sighed when the couple finally overcame all their problems, and it looked like they would get back together. Clancy declared he would never eat Angel's cooking, since Julia Roberts, who played the wife, had made the unfaithful husband sick by putting ipecac in his food.

"You don't have to worry about it, Clancy. I don't cook," she said.

"But—but—" he stammered. "You are so good at everything. I figured you'd be a gourmet cook. I mean, you play golf. You run an oil company, and even Red stands in awe of you."

"I don't cook. Really and truly. I do not cook," she answered. "Granny did the cooking when she was alive. And she did a fine job, so I didn't need to know how. Then when she died, I learned I could live on cans of pork and beans and wieners from the grocery store. By the time I got tired of that menu, I was in the oil business. Hilda cooks for me, and she does a fine job. I suppose you won't ever call me for a second date now, will you?"

"That's where you are wrong." He picked up a bread-stick and dipped it in marinara sauce. "I can cook. There are restaurants on every corner no matter where you go. Cooks can be hired."

Angel yawned. "That's pretty much what I think."

"Sleepy?" Clancy asked.

"A little," Angel answered. "Watch whatever you want. Just wake me early enough so I can get dressed and do something with my hair before it's time to leave," she said as she closed her eyes.

"Good night, Angel," he said as he slid off the side of the bed, put all the leftovers on the desk, and got into his own bed.

"Night, Clance," she mumbled.

⸻

That she called him Clance, as she'd done when they were meeting at the sandbar in Tishomingo, didn't merely go over the top of his head. Sure, she was sleepy and tired, and it could have been just a slip of the tongue, but it meant something to Clancy.

He watched a couple of reruns of *NCIS*, but he didn't remember much of it. All he could think about was Angel, sleeping soundly beside him in the next bed. He wondered what it would be like to see her face the first thing every morning. He made a trip to the bathroom and stopped by her bed. He bent and brushed a sweet kiss across her lips.

"Clance," she mumbled.

"Good night, Angel," he whispered softly in her ear.

Before he could straighten up, she wrapped her arms around him and pulled his mouth down to hers for a searing kiss.

"I told you..." She sat straight up in bed, eyes wide open.

"Hey..." He backed up and put up his hands like the victim in an Old West bank robbery. "You started it. I just stole one little kiss and said good night."

"Oh, I must have been dreaming," she remembered. "We were..." she stammered. "Never mind." She looked bewildered.

"Never mind what?" he pressed.

"This is crazy, Clancy." She sat and patted the bed beside her.

He sat down and took her hand in his. She reached out to touch the soft hair on his chest where the silk bathrobe parted, and the thrill of it inched up and down his spine.

"Kiss me again. This time for real," she said.

"Are you sure about this?" Clancy asked.

She pulled his mouth down to hers in a passionate kiss.

"Angel…" His low voice was almost a growl.

━━━━━━

"Crawl in here with me." She pulled the covers back and invited him into her bed. Tomorrow she might be sorry. But tonight, she was going to make love with Clancy Morgan, and the devil could have tomorrow. The future was a blur, the past was a mistake, but the present was theirs. Angel wanted to feel his body next to hers like she had on those hot summer nights a decade ago.

There was no hurry. Neither of them was eighteen years old nor did they have to be home by midnight. They enjoyed long, exploring kisses until they were breathless. Clancy undressed her slowly, and the whole world stood still while they rediscovered each other's bodies.

Afterward, she curled up to sleep in his arms and he drew her close to his side. *Was that closure?* she asked herself as she drifted off to sleep. *Or was it another heartache waiting to happen?*

Angel awoke with a start when the alarm on her phone buzzed at seven o'clock. She was still in the crook of Clancy's arm, snuggled up beside him. Lord, what had she done? This was all her own doing. She'd made the first overture so she couldn't blame what happened on him. Before she could get anything sorted out, he opened his eyes, smiled, and kept staring at her, making little ripples travel up and down her spine.

"Good morning," he finally said when she didn't blink her green eyes. "Regrets?"

She shook her head. "Not a single one." *But you might have some when we get to Tishomingo,* she thought. *A fling out here on the road is one thing. But Tishomingo is home, and nothing much changes there, except who's on the hot seat when it comes to the rumors.*

"Me either," he said and changed the subject. "This is Friday. We could give ourselves plenty of time and get home on Saturday night. Want to stop off in Shreveport and play on a gambling boat tonight, or go dancing?"

"Let's go as far as Shreveport and rent a motel room with one bed," she said seriously.

Clancy eyed her closely. "Are you serious?"

"Yes, I am," she answered. "But first, I'm having cold pizza for breakfast."

She threw the sheets back, picked up her clothes, and

headed to the bathroom. "Save me a piece of that Hawaiian. It's better than I thought it would be."

"I'll make a couple of cups of coffee. Decaf?" he asked.

"Nope, high octane and nothing in it. I'll be out as soon as I tame this hair. How far is it to Shreveport?" she asked.

"Too far." He chuckled.

Chapter 13

"Maybe this isn't a good idea." Angel felt like she had dozens of butterflies the size of buzzards flapping their wings in her stomach. She hadn't been this nervous since the day she signed the final papers to purchase the building for Conrad Oil.

"Hey, it's all right, I promise." Clancy shut the door of his Bronco and went around to open her door and gather up a load of luggage. "My mother doesn't bite, you know. And besides, she and Tom are still honeymooners so they won't even know we're around most of the time."

"You should have called first. She can't say no now." Angel nervously tugged her red shorts down and smoothed the front of a matching sleeveless shirt.

"Clancy!" Meredith Morgan, immaculately groomed as

always, met them at the front door. "And Angela? Is that really you all grown up? Come in. Tom and I just got home this morning. We've been watching for you since you called yesterday morning."

"We thought we'd move into the guesthouse out by the pool if that's all right," Clancy said as he walked in the front door and set the bags down to hug his mother. "Angel's still got the better part of two weeks' vacation," he explained.

Angel looked around at the inside of the house. It hadn't changed much since the last time she was there with her granny. The only thing new was the pool and guesthouse, which she could see through double glass sliding doors on the other side of the dining area.

"Hello." She stuck her hand out to Meredith when Clancy set the luggage down in the living room and went back for the rest.

"Oh, don't you offer me that hand, girl. Come here and give me a hug. I'm so sorry to hear about your grandmother's passing." Meredith wrapped her arms around Angel and patted her back. "She was a fine woman and a good friend. Now, tell me about that storm. I'm glad you got out in time. We were really worried until Clancy called us."

"We didn't have service for hours and hours," Angel

answered. "I didn't know if Clancy was going to drive us out or paddle us out for a while there, but we finally reached dry ground. Are you sure this is all right? I can get a motel room."

"This is fine. We're glad to have you." Meredith brushed away the idea with a flick of her hand. "That's what the guesthouse was built for. The pool isn't the ocean, but I bet the sun's just as hot here, and you won't have to worry about a storm."

"Thanks." Angel nodded. "Clancy, honey, let me help you take our things out to the guesthouse."

"This way." He nodded toward the doors about the same time Tom opened them from the outside.

"Merrie," he said, "those ferns have got to be watered every day, and we're going to have to plant more... Oh, hello, Clancy. Glad you kids made it home." He grinned. "Oh my goodness! Angel Conrad! Come here and give me a hug, child. Lord, it's been ten years since I've seen you, and you're more beautiful than ever. You're a lucky man, Clancy!"

"You're still a giant." She giggled, standing on her tiptoes to hug him.

"And you haven't grown an inch!" Tom grinned. "Are you stayin' awhile with us?"

"I guess so. The storm sent us back home, and Clancy says there's room for me in the guesthouse."

"Room for you anywhere you want to hang your hat around here," Tom said. "Let me carry those bags for you. We've got dinner reservations at some place over in Ardmore. You two have to go with us." He skirted the pool and opened the west door of the guest cottage.

Meredith was behind him, shaking her head. Tom couldn't see it, but Clancy and Angel could.

"Thanks, Tom," Angel said. "But it's been a long day, and all I want is a hamburger from the Dairy Queen. Then I want to come back here and sit in one of those lounge chairs by the pool until the stars come out. Airplanes were meant to get a person from one end of this country to the other, not automobiles!"

"I heard that." Tom set the suitcases inside the guesthouse and then backed out the door. "Y'all make yourselves at home. I'll go on in the house and get ready to go, and you kids can fend for yourselves. And, Angel, it's mighty good to have you back for a while. We missed you and your granny when you left."

"Thank you." She flashed a bright, honest smile toward him.

"Not that I don't want you," Meredith whispered, "but this is a special evening I had planned for the two of us…"

"We understand," Angel said.

"You are going to church with us in the morning, aren't you? The service begins at eleven," she said.

"Sure." Clancy nodded. "We'll be up and ready, Mama."

Meredith closed the door behind her, and Clancy turned to Angel, wrapped her in his arms, and kissed her. "See, I told you," he whispered.

"Okay, you win," Angel said. *But that doesn't mean this whole experience is going to be one, big happy ending to our love story*, she thought.

An hour later, Clancy held open the door of the local Dairy Queen for her, then chose a table for two right in the middle of the restaurant. While he went to the counter to order hamburgers, she remembered what she'd thought about on the beach. She had expected to be impressed if he took her to the Dairy Queen on Main Street in Tishomingo, and here she was, but the sun hadn't fallen from the sky, and she didn't feel like a queen who had just been given the Hope Diamond. The event that would have made her swoon at the age of eighteen wasn't such a big deal at the age of twenty-eight!

"Hey, Clancy!" The voice of Jim Moore, an old classmate of theirs, boomed from two tables over. "Where you been, man? We got up a fishing trip last night down on the river and caught a ton of suckers. Larry fried them on the river-bank and brought the beer. You missed a good time."

"We were busy outrunning that tropical storm down in Florida." Clancy grinned at his old friend.

"We?" Jim raised an eyebrow. "You and Melissa getting back together?"

"Hell no!" Clancy exclaimed.

"Oh, hi, Clancy." Janie came through the side door and walked up beside her husband. "You didn't order for me, did you?" she asked. "You seen Melissa?"

"Yep, and I don't ever want to see her again," he answered. He motioned to his friends. "Get your food and come sit with us." Clancy nodded toward the center of the room.

"Sure," Jim said. "What do you want, Janie? Bacon cheeseburger with extra cheese?"

"Not with all those fat grams!" She slapped his arm. "Give me a chef's salad and a Diet Coke."

Angel smiled up at Clancy when he set a tray with their burgers in the middle of the table. "Since you've provided our supper, I'll wash the dishes when we finish, just to show you I'm all for equality."

He threw back his head and laughed. "Does that mean you'll tote the paper to the trash can and put the tray on the shelf above it?"

"Yep, and don't take it lightly, sir. I don't offer to do dishes very often." Angel unwrapped her burger. "I love junk food. Beats cooking any day."

"Clancy, have you heard about Melissa?" Janie pulled up a chair and sat down, then turned to focus on Angel. "I don't think we've met, but you sure look familiar." She squinted until the crow's-feet around her blue eyes deepened. "Good God! You're Angela Conrad."

"Yes, I am," Angel said. "We graduated from high school together."

Janie looked like she'd been hit with a crowbar right between the eyes. "Are you and Clancy... But Melissa is..." Her words came out one at a time, and she kept looking from Clancy to Angel. "When did this happen?"

"We dated in high school between our senior year and when I went to college," Clancy answered. "We reunited after the alumni reunion."

"But Melissa..." Janie frowned. "She says that..."

Clancy raised a palm. "I'd rather not talk about her." He removed the paper from his burger and took a bite.

Jim brought their food and set it down. "What did I miss?"

"That I'm dating Angel," Clancy answered.

Janie stared down at her salad. "But Melissa and Daniel are getting a divorce, and now's the perfect time for you two to mend the fences and get back together." Then she looked up and glared at Angel.

If looks could kill, Angel would be stretched out on the floor, ready for the undertaker to embalm her. Janie and Melissa had been inseparable in high school, and evidently, their friendship was still as strong as ever.

Angel picked up her hamburger and forced herself to eat a bite even though the burger had lost some of its taste.

Janie turned back to Clancy and ignored Angel. "Melissa told me she was going to Florida to see you and that you two might work things out," she said, as if Angel were just another piece of furniture. "Then she called and said she was flying to Virginia to settle things there, so I thought—"

"Evidently you thought wrong," Jim interrupted. "It's good to see you, Angela. Where have you been keeping yourself all these years?"

"Oh, I live in Kemp part of the time and in Denison the rest," Angel answered.

"What are you doin'? Besides outrunnin' storms and singin' with that band of yours." Jim picked up his chili dog and took a bite.

"She's the president of Conrad Oil Enterprises," Clancy answered.

"You're kiddin'." Jim's eyes were as round as saucers. "You are that Angel? Red talks about you all the time. Says you're smarter'n anybody in the business. Lord, I didn't know he was talkin' about Angela Conrad."

"Thank you," she said. "How do you know Red?"

Janie picked at her salad as if she expected to find a cockroach hidden under the lettuce leaves.

"I've been workin' for him eight years now," Jim said. "Lots of us here in Tish commute together down to the offshore rigs. Out two weeks, home two weeks. Janie loves half of it." He grinned. "That would be the half I'm gone."

"Oh, hush!" Janie almost growled at him. "It's just I can't get anything done with him home twenty-four hours a day for two weeks." She continued to ignore Angel. "He's always underfoot somehow. I just talked to Melissa again today. She'll be back in town, maybe even tonight or tomorrow. I've invited her to stay with me."

Clancy reached over and draped an arm around Angel's

shoulders. "Let's get something straight right now, Janie. Melissa and I are history. She's the one who wanted a divorce so she could marry someone else. I'm not interested in a rematch. She needs to get on with her life."

"Oh, sure, you'd say that. You're running from your responsibilities. If you'd been a decent husband, then she wouldn't have left you." Janie flared up at him. "Melissa told me she was pregnant and going to Florida to tell you. Evidently she found you there with Angela."

"The baby is not mine." Clancy said through gritted teeth. Then he chuckled. That soon turned into a guffaw. "This is so damned funny. It should feed the gossip mill here in town for weeks."

"Are you crazy?" Jim stared at him.

"Not me!" Clancy wiped his eyes. "It's the rest of the world that's crazy. You're crazy, Janie." Clancy leaned forward until his nose was just inches from hers. "Melissa may be pregnant. That's her business. The baby might be Daniel's or someone else's. That's still her problem and her life to sort out. If she told you I got her pregnant, then your best friend lied to you. If the two of you hatched up this scheme together, then you know I'm telling the truth."

"Well, if it weren't for you"—Janie spun around and

stared at Angela—"Clancy and Melissa might work things out. They belong together."

"Janie, why don't you shut up?" Jim asked softly. "This ain't your business."

"Yes, it is." She turned on him. "Melissa's been my best friend since we were three years old. So, she made a big mistake by leaving Clancy for Daniel. So, she got pregnant and her husband's not the father, but—" Janie clamped a hand over her mouth and blushed.

"Just exactly who is the baby daddy?" Angela asked.

"Oh, go to hell. You never did belong to our crowd and you won't now, just because he's got blinders on," Janie hissed. "Don't think we'll all welcome you with open arms just because you slept your way to the top of some oil company, and Clancy thinks you're hot stuff."

"Who's the father, Janie?" Jim asked, suddenly interested in the story. "Clancy says it's none of his doing, and I believe him. If I was him, I damned sure wouldn't be fool enough to remarry her. You treat me like Melissa's treated him and I'll boot your backside out the door, woman."

Angel bit back a grin and took another bite of her burger. Janie was entitled to her own opinion. She didn't care that Melissa had been hateful. Angel dealt with rude people every day. What mattered was that Angel hadn't let her emotions lead her down the wrong road. Angel Conrad was a force to be reckoned with. She lacked neither security nor self-esteem, and these days she wasn't afraid to stand up for what she wanted and fight for it.

"I'm goin' home," Janie stood up so fast she knocked her chair backward on the floor, and glared at Jim. "And you can either go with me or sleep on the river bank tonight in your fishin' tent."

Jim didn't even look up at her. "I'm finishin' this chili dog, Janie, and the riverbanks will be a nicer place to sleep than your bed. I'll be by the house and get my things tomorrow to go out for two weeks, and then you can keep things wonder-ful and clean."

"I'll be glad to see you leave," she said through clenched teeth.

"Maybe, but I can't believe you would try to hogswoggle our friend into marryin' Melissa when that baby ain't his kid. What were you thinkin', Janie? That you and Melissa would laugh behind his back about it? I'm ashamed of you." He finally looked up at her.

"Melissa is my friend, and Angela, you are a bitch," Janie whispered and stormed out the door toward her bright-red car.

Angel stood up slowly and started toward the door. Clancy rolled his eyes and started to get up, too, but Jim put his hand on his friend's arm and held him down. "Don't. Let them alone. It's high time my wife found out she can't act like a horse's ass and get away with it."

Angel turned around and nodded. "He's right, Clancy. I can take care of myself."

―――――――

"I think we better straighten something out." Angel opened the passenger door to Janie's car and slid into it.

"Get out of my car, you bitch!" Janie screamed at her. "Right now."

"I'm going to talk, and although you might not like it, you will listen," Angel said calmly, as if she was talking to a child. "If you want to drive away, that's okay. Everyone in town can see you with me in the car, and you can explain that to Melissa when you talk to her again. Maybe they'll even put it in the 'Seen' column on the front page of the newspaper next week. 'Seen: Angel Conrad and Janie Moore enjoying an evening ride down Main Street.'" On the outside, Angel was as unruffled as a freshly made bed. Inside, she was a boiling cauldron of rage.

"You're going to get out of my car, or I'm going to throw you out," Janie threatened.

"Stop acting like a teenager," Angel told her. "We're adults now, Janie. We're not in grade school, and this is not a little red wagon you won't let me ride in. We're grown women. You're entitled to your opinion, and if you don't like me, that's fine."

"What?" Janie gasped.

"I was there when Melissa tried to snag Clancy into another marriage because she's desperate and needs a husband, and he was always dependable. She just didn't figure on me being there when she arrived. There's no excuse for such a low-down, dirty trick, although you can be her friend and help her scheme if you want to. That's your prerogative." Angel looked the woman right in the eye and loved it when Janie began to squirm.

"I deal with people who don't like me every day, Janie. That's life in the real world. I made a big mistake ten years ago and didn't listen to my heart when it told me Clancy was bad news. I'm sure Melissa told you about my son. He was stillborn, and he looked so much like Clancy that it broke my heart all over again to see him in that little blue casket. But that's Clancy's and my business, not yours. I followed you out here to tell you two things. One is that you better not push that husband of yours too far, or you'll be living on whatever you can make along with a child-support check. The second is that you'd better never call me a bitch again—or I'll mop up the streets of this little town with you. I'm not from around here, and I don't really care what people think anymore. Have a nice night, Janie, and when you go to sleep all alone tonight, remember it could be permanent!"

Angel opened the door.

"Wait!" Janie said. Tears began to stream down her cheeks. "Do you really think Jim would leave me?"

"There are lots of women out there who would fall all over themselves to get a chance at a hardworking, good-looking man like Jim Moore." Angel closed the door. "You know who that baby belongs to, don't you?"

Janie nodded. "But Melissa knows so many of my secrets that..."

"A best friend wouldn't blackmail you, girl. You need to ask yourself which is more important to you. Your marriage or your friendship?" Angel said.

"She had a couple of abortions when she was married to Clancy, and she's afraid to have another one. I shouldn't be telling you this. She's my friend."

"I knew the baby wasn't Clancy's, and that's all that's important to me," Angel said. "The rest is her business, and yours if you decide to choose her over Jim. You have a nice rest of the evening."

"Thanks." Janie wiped the tears away with the back of her hand. "I needed someone to set me straight. I'm going to call Melissa and tell her that she needs to stay somewhere else when she gets into town."

"Again, that's your business, not mine." This time Angel got out of the car and went back into the Dairy Queen. She slid into the chair beside Clancy and stuck a straw into her milkshake.

"No blood or broken bones, I hope," Clancy said.

"Wouldn't blame you if there was," Jim muttered.

"Nope." Angel smiled. "We just had a come-to-Jesus talk. I think she might want to talk to you, Jim. Go on out there. Betcha she's ready to tell you she's sorry," Angela said.

"Sure, when hell freezes over," Jim snorted, but he got up and left.

"Good food, Clancy. Thanks. Not such good company for a little while there, but that's changed now and the company is as good as the food," Angel said. "When we get done, let's go to the creek where the old swinging bridge used to be and sit on the banks in the grass and see if any ducks float by. There used to be a few when I was a little girl. Granny cleaned a couple of houses over there, and I was terrified of that little footbridge back then."

Clancy nodded, but it was plain that his attention wasn't on an old footbridge that crossed Pennington Creek. "What'd you say to Janie?" he asked. "They just drove off, and Jim waved and winked at me."

"Not much. I told Janie a few things she needed to hear about Jim."

"And?"

"Oh, all right. I said that I didn't appreciate being called a bitch, and I told her what I intended to do if she called me that again. And that she needed to figure out what was more important, her marriage or her friendship with Melissa."

"So, you are a therapist too?" Clancy teased.

"No, sir!" Angel answered. "I'm just a woman who saw a problem and told an old classmate about it."

Chapter 14

CLANCY STOPPED IN THE MIDDLE OF THE NEW CONCRETE bridge that had replaced the old swinging bridge a flood had wiped out years and years ago. "Daddy used to tease Mama about the old bridge. When they were dating, he would speed out to the middle of the bridge and then brake so the bridge would sway back and forth. Mama would scream, and he'd draw her into his arms and comfort her."

"I don't have memories of my folks. They were truck drivers and left me with Granny for weeks on end. When they got killed, I was only three years old," she said.

"I'm sorry," Clancy whispered as he drove the rest of the way across the bridge and parked on the edge of the road near the creek.

"It is what it is. Granny was a wonderful mother to me,"

Angel said. "Looks like the ducks have all gone to roost for the night."

"We can get out and sit on the sandbar. It's not as wide as the one at the dam, but we can sit out there and listen to the crickets and tree frogs," Clancy said.

She didn't wait for him to come around and open the door for her but got out of his Bronco and plopped down on the grass. She removed her sandals and stretched her legs out so her toes were in the narrow bit of sand by the water. Sure enough, she could hear crickets and tree frogs blending their voices together to make a fine concert.

"You know, for years, I fantasized about the day you would take me to the Dairy Queen and we'd walk in looking like two people in love. I expected it to be the most wonderful day in the whole world." She picked up a stick and drew two hearts in the wet sand. They touched but they didn't overlap. "That last night we were together and I told you about the baby, I had drawn a couple of entwined hearts in the sand and wrote 'baby' in the part where they joined."

"I'm sorry," he whispered as he sat down close to her.

The night breeze brought a whiff of his cologne to her, and she inhaled deeply. "Don't be sorry. Tonight, I realized that if we would have done things differently then, we wouldn't be the people we are today. What I feel for you today is much stronger than it was ten years ago, Clancy. If you had given up your hopes and dreams then, you might have resented me. I'm not totally sure we would have stayed together. Very few teenage marriages, especially those that start out because of a pregnancy, ever last."

"You're right again." He scooted over closer to her and kissed her on the cheek. "Want to go home and take a moonlight swim?"

"Sure." Angel hopped up, took a final look at the two hearts, and didn't kick sand over them this time.

The drive from one end of town to the other took all of five minutes, and that was even stopping at the two traffic lights. When they reached the guesthouse, Clancy swept her up like a bride and carried her into the small bedroom.

"I thought this kind of thing was saved for a wedding night," Angel said, giggling.

"You and I do things different than most people." He grinned as he set her down on the floor. "Swim or..." He waggled his eyebrows.

"I kind of like that 'or' business," she told him as she untucked his shirt and tugged at the bottom to undo all the snaps in one fell swoop.

He cupped her cheeks in his hands and kissed her, and at the same time kicked the door shut with his bootheel. "'Or' has always been a favorite of mine," Clancy said as he walked her backward to the edge of the bed.

━━━━━━

Angel dived into the water and decided that the next thing on her list for the farm was a swimming pool. She didn't know why she hadn't thought of it before now. She had always loved water, and sometimes she even rented a hotel room and stayed in the city just so she could have a swim.

When she came up at the end of the pool, she saw Tom stretched out in a chaise lounge with his feet propped up. "Hey, I thought you two kids were tuckered out."

"Not me." Angel giggled. "I could swim forever. Race you to the other end, Clancy," she said and started before he even got into the water.

"You cheated," he accused when she beat him.

She shook her head. "All's fair in love and war."

"That's the gospel truth." Meredith sat down beside Tom in a second chaise lounge and reached across the space to take his hand. "We had a great time. Tom even danced with me. He's not too bad on his feet." She smiled. "Surprised me to be swept around the floor in a perfect waltz. When we were in San Antonio, he told me that he couldn't dance at all."

Tom winked at Clancy. "Only stepped on her feet a few times."

"Y'all still goin' to church with us?" Meredith asked. "Be up and around by eleven if you are. We've invited a bunch of friends for a poolside lunch afterward. Nothing too big. Sandwiches and a small wedding cake. The photographer will take a few pictures so we can show the grandchildren some-day...we hope." She directed a smile toward Clancy.

"We'll be up and around." Clancy nodded. "Maybe the photographer can shoot a few of me and Angel," he suggested.

Angel propped her arms on the edge of the pool. "If my hair cooperates in the morning, I'd be willing for that."

The next morning, Clancy arrived in the kitchen at ten o'clock, wiping sleep from his eyes and yawning. He wore a pair of his oldest shorts and a faded purple muscle shirt he usually used for fishing. "Mornin', Mama." He gave her a quick hug and headed toward the coffeepot. "Tom up yet?"

"He's shaving," Meredith said. "And while I've got you alone, I have a couple of things to say. First of all, if you let

Angel get away from you this time, you'll regret it forever. That girl is so much in love with you it's written all over her. And what's this I hear about Janie insulting her yesterday? Did you take care of it?"

Clancy shook his head. "Didn't have to. Angel did. Do you really think she loves me?" He sipped the coffee and opened his eyes wide. "Hey, how did you know about Janie's snit?"

"Doesn't take the gossip line long to get hot. June called me this morning about the cake and said Janie told her mother she and Angel had words. This is a small town, and you've got to be able to trace your ancestry all the way back to Noah before you're important around here. But I'm worried about Angel."

Clancy put his hand up. "I love her with all my heart. I just don't want to rush things. I'd marry her tomorrow, but I'm going to court her properly and then propose just like in the movies, on one knee with a big diamond in my pocket. Then if she wants a wedding big enough for Texas with all those women who were in her band standing beside her and a reception that lasts six days and nights, we'll have it. This time, my Angel is going to have everything I was too young and insecure to offer her ten years ago."

Meredith waggled a finger at him. "Don't forget stupid."

"Thanks a lot for reminding me, but even that can't take away my happiness this morning." Clancy chuckled.

"Fine." Meredith smiled. "Get on out there and wake your fiancée up, even though she doesn't know she's going to marry you just yet. Take her a cup of coffee and a bagel. And let me tell you, Son, if I hear anyone putting her down, they'd better be ready for a first-rate catfight. She's the best damned thing that's happened to you in a long time. I can't even remember the last time your eyes had such a bright light in them."

"Don't I know it!" He filled two mugs with coffee and set them on a tray along with bagels, cream cheese, and a bowl of fresh fruit Meredith had cut up for breakfast. Then he carefully carried the tray out the patio door.

"Good mornin', darlin'," he said as he walked into the guesthouse. "I'm carrying hot coffee. Don't be grabbing my arm and dragging me into your room for a wild, passionate love-a-thon right now. We need sustenance if we're going to keep up this pace."

"Well, I do need to build up my energy before I tackle my hair this morning." Angel grinned as she picked up a mug of coffee and carried it over to the love seat.

He set the tray on the coffee table and sat down beside her.

"Why does it take so long to do your hair?" Clancy asked. "I love it just the way it is, all curly with a sprig or two hanging in your eyes."

"You want to walk into church with me looking like I just crawled out of bed?" she asked as she spread cream cheese on a bagel and held it out to him to take a bite.

"I'd rather stay right here and go back to bed with you if I have a choice." He bit off a piece of the bagel. "Do you feed all the guys you go to bed with?"

"Only the ones that I let spend the night," she answered.

"And how many would that be?" he asked.

"How many women have spent the night with you in this guesthouse?" she asked.

"One," he answered as he picked up a strawberry and fed it to her.

"Melissa?" she asked.

"No, Mama didn't have the pool or guesthouse until after we'd divorced. You're the only one I've ever brought here," he answered.

"I've never let a guy spend the night in either my apartment in Denison or at my farm," she answered. "And that's all I've got to say about that."

"Fair enough. Let's leave the past in the past, and, honey,

if you just want to twist your hair up in one of those bun things this morning, or any morning as far as that goes, I think you're beautiful with a hairdo like that," he said.

"But you mentioned pictures," she said. "Don't you want to be proud of the woman standing beside you?"

"I'd be proud of you if you were wearing a faded red bikini and no makeup," he told her.

———————

Angel knew there would be lots of familiar faces at the church, but she wouldn't have to make small talk with anyone for more than a few minutes after the services. The reception would be a different matter. Whether she liked it or not, she'd feel just like she did in high school. All those people would realize she was that poor little girl from the wrong side of the tracks, and they'd pity Clancy. She remembered the line from an old country song by Cross Canadian Ragweed, "17."

The lyrics talked about always being the same person in a hometown as you were when you were there as a teenager. That a person had made something of themselves didn't matter a whole lot—folks still remembered them as whatever they were in high school. Maybe that's why folks who had been popular never left. They didn't want to lose that feeling of being slightly better than everyone else.

Angel forced herself not to think about the song. She wasn't the same girl, and she'd show everyone she was confident and independent. "Are you sure you want pictures of us?"

"Positive," he said without hesitation.

"All right, then," she said. "Then I'm going to work on my hair a little bit. Granny said that I got this kinky stuff from my father, not my mother. Most days I'd like to give it right back to him."

"Honey, I wouldn't change a single thing about you." He leaned over and kissed her on the cheek.

When you get ready to settle down, you find a man who loves you just the way you are and doesn't want to change you to suit what he wants. Her grandmother's words came back to her as she finished off her bagel.

They made it to church just moments before the morning services began. Angel felt many eyes on her as she walked down the aisle holding Clancy's hand, but she held her head high and her back straight. She had dressed that morning in a bright floral sundress and red sandals and had brought along a lightweight sweater in case it was chilly in the church.

Clancy's eyes told her she was beautiful, so she didn't give a tiny rat's hind end what anyone else thought of her.

That's my girl! She could almost feel her grandmother hugging her right there in the church.

"Is that Dillon Williamson?" she whispered when she sat down between Meredith and Clancy. The preacher looked like the guy who graduated with them, but it was hard to imagine that kid ever growing up to be a preacher—not even if she stretched her imagination all the way to the breaking point. Evidently, he wasn't always seventeen in his hometown.

"Yes, it is. This is his first year to pastor this church," Clancy answered.

Dillon had graduated just a year after Clancy and Angel, and he was the wildest boy in high school. To see him in a three-piece suit up there on the short bench behind the lectern was a shock to say the least. Angel kept staring at him, still not believing her eyes.

The song leader smiled at everyone, cleared his throat, and said, "Welcome to everyone this mornin', especially to Tom and Meredith who just got back from their honeymoon and to Clancy and Angel, both of whom went to school with me right here in Tishomingo. Now, please turn to page 181 in your hymnals, and we'll have congregational singing."

Angel could practically hear the buzz of gossip over the top of the singing. Angela Conrad had come back to Tishomingo, and Clancy was sharing a hymnal with her. Why, that was right next door to being engaged!

After they had finished the song, the preacher stepped up to the lectern and preached from Matthew about the Sermon on the Mount, and Angela could almost feel the heat rising from the pews when he came to the part about judging one's neighbor. Then she realized that she'd done just that. She had already decided what people's attitudes toward her would be before she had even talked to them. Granny would be disappointed in her for attending services with a chip on her shoulder.

Leave all your worries and cares at the door when you go to church. Those had been Granny's words. *God is the only one you have to think about when you're sitting in his place of worship. What others think, what they're wearing, or who they're sitting with is none of your business. You have come to meet with God.*

Clancy reached across his lap to hold her left hand and draped his right arm around her. *I hear you loud and clear, Granny.* A smile tickled the corners of her mouth. *But it's kind of hard to keep my mind on God or the sermon with Clancy this close.*

When Dillon finished his sermon, he asked Tom to deliver the benediction. Tom stood up, bowed his head, and thanked God for the wonderful day, for good fellowship, and for the love that bound the church family together.

Angel took an extra second after he had said the final amen to give thanks for giving her a second chance with Clancy. When she opened her eyes, several folks were gathering around Tom and Meredith to congratulate them. Afterward, many of them shook her hand and told her how good it was to see her again. By the time the four of them left the church, they were the last ones to shake hands with the preacher.

"Angela Conrad, I remember you. You were super smart, much too intelligent to be hanging around this guy." He grinned at Clancy.

"I don't know about all that. I hear from a friend of mine that he's wasting his talents on teaching," Angel said.

"Helping people is never a waste," Dillon said. "You come on back to see us again. We're glad to have you."

"Thank you, and it's good to be back for a visit."

"You ready for this?" Clancy asked as he opened the back door of his mother's Cadillac for Angel to get into the vehicle.

"Are you?" she asked.

"Oh, yeah." He slid in beside her and took her hand in

his. "I couldn't be more ready to show the whole town what a lucky guy I am."

If Angel was sleeping, she damn sure didn't want anyone to wake her up. "Smile pretty," she said as she held up her cell phone and took a selfie of the two of them. Then she sent it to all five of her friends with a note: *We haven't killed each other, and I'm staying until my two weeks are up.*

Tom parked in the garage, and the four of them went out onto the patio through the back door. "Oh my!" Angel gasped. "I thought this was going to be just a small affair."

"We didn't invite the whole town, even though it kind of looks that way," Meredith assured her with a hug. "It's just that we have so many friends that we didn't want to leave anyone out."

Lace cloths covered round tables that had been arranged around the pool. Bouquets of fresh roses and daisies decorated the middle of each table, already set with silver wrapped in crisp white linen napkins. Just outside the dining-room doors, a long table held barbecued brisket, chicken, and ribs, baked beans and potato salad, along with several trays of fresh fruit, cheese, and raw vegetables. The three-tiered wedding cake, topped with a pair of porcelain lovebirds sitting in an orange blossom nest, was the centerpiece for the longest table, with a silver coffee service on one end and a matching punch bowl on the other.

"This looks pretty formal to me," Angel whispered to Clancy. "I should change into the only party dress I brought along. I didn't think I'd be needing anything formal at the beach. Or Tishomingo."

"You look fabulous." Clancy gave her a hug and kissed her on the forehead.

"Thank you"—she smiled—"but I wasn't fishing for compliments. I was serious."

"I know a beautiful woman when I see one." Clancy kept his arm around her shoulders. "I thought I was going to die before I could get another kiss. It seemed like Dillon preached for hours this morning, and then all those folks wanting to talk to Mama and see you again. I was feeling pretty puny."

"Clancy, you are full of bull—"

He put his fingers over her mouth. "Here comes Wilma Jones. If she hears you say that entire word, she'll drop down on her knees and commence to praying for your soul right here and now," he whispered in mock seriousness, then turned abruptly. "Oh, hello, Mrs. Jones. Do you remember Angela Conrad? She lived here when we were in high school." Clancy brought Angel around to stand beside him with his arm still around her shoulder.

"Nope, can't say as I do." Mrs. Jones shook her head. "Pretty woman, though, Clancy. If you had half a brain, you'd keep her close to you. There's some bachelors in the crowd who are already eyeing her. Now, where is your mother? I want to offer my congratulations. Some folks is talking about her marryin' up with Tom, but they're just jealous because they don't have someone to treat them that good." The old woman shook her finger under his nose as if she were preaching him a sermon.

"Whew, close call." Angel giggled when Mrs. Jones was out of hearing distance. "I like Mrs. Jones. She says what she thinks."

"Yep, she does. Don't you remember her from church when we were in school?"

"Clancy, I didn't go to your church. I went with my granny to the Methodist church over on the other side of town," she reminded him.

People continued to arrive for half an hour and milled around among the tables, visiting as they waited for Sunday dinner to be served. Several stopped by to be introduced to Angel. Some remembered her vaguely; others didn't. But in a while, she began to feel more comfortable. Then Tom clapped his hands three times to get everyone's attention.

"Merrie and I want to thank you for coming to share this special time with us." He smiled. "We're glad you are here. I know you're all hungry and we appreciate you waitin' while the photographer snapped a few pictures of us. He's got a real strong camera. My ugly mug didn't even break it! Now, let's all form a line right here and start eating." He took Meredith's hand in his and led her to the food table.

"Clancy!" his mother called to him across the pool. "The photographer is waiting for you and Angel inside. I told him to take a bunch of you two." She pointed through the glass doors.

"Let me freshen my makeup and lipstick. I'll just be a minute," Angel said. She headed toward the bathroom, and when she passed the den, she heard her name. She stopped and flattened her back against the wall beside the open door.

"Janie told me that Melissa was pregnant," one of the trio said. "And it's not her husband's baby. She went down to Florida to try to get Clancy to marry her again, but she found Angel down there with him. I hope his mother knows what Clancy is getting into."

"Oh, Meredith's got her head so far up in the clouds, she

wouldn't know straight up from backwards right now," the second one said.

"Don't knock it!" the third woman added tartly. "I've lived alone ever since my Frank died, and I don't like it. If I'd known Tom Lloyd was lookin' for a wife, I would've been out at that cemetery so fast it would look like a tornado headed that way. Meredith is a good woman and she was a good wife to that first husband of hers. He was a good man but a whole lot on the uppity side. Can you imagine the late Mr. Morgan out there on his knees doin' yard work or lookin' at Meredith like she was a queen? Lord, I'd lay down on the freeway and die a happy woman for just one day of a good man lookin' at me like that."

"Don't change the subject. Do you really think Melissa and Clancy are through?" The first voice sounded incredulous.

"Of course they are! They shouldn't ever have gotten married in the first place. I don't remember Angela much. I think she was one of those kids who just blended in with the background in high school, but she sure doesn't now. I'd love to have that figure she's got, and I hear she owns an oil company. That probably makes her the most prosperous kid to ever come out of Tishomingo High School," the lady said.

Angel stifled a giggle.

"In my opinion, Melissa has gone too far," a third voice piped up. "She's been a spoiled brat her whole life. It's time for her to be accountable. We'd better get on out to the reception before the food is all gone. Those women with husbands should be through the line now and us old widow women can have what's left." She stood up and Angel barely had time to go on down the hall and get the bathroom door shut before she heard them making their way down the hallway.

She checked the mirror and was only slightly surprised to see two round spots of color on her cheeks. It had been a long time since anyone or anything made her blush. She reapplied her lipstick and went back to the living room where Clancy waited patiently.

The photographer looked across the room and smiled. "I don't often get to take pictures of such a beautiful couple."

Angel blushed. "Thank you, sir. Just tell us what to do."

"How about here by the fireplace? And I'm just plain old Greg, no 'sir.'" He pointed toward the fireplace. "Clancy, would you please stand behind her and put your arms around her waist?"

"Gladly," Clancy said.

"Now, lean back just slightly, Angel," Greg said. "Tilt

your head just a little. Now look at me with those big, green eyes and don't smile," he said.

And Angel smiled.

"Works every time." He snapped several shots, checked them on the camera, and nodded. "Let's go over to that antique chair. You sit down, Angel. Clancy, stand behind her with your hands on her shoulders."

"When we get done with this one, can we have one of Angel sitting in my lap?" Clancy asked.

"Anything you want," Greg agreed.

Angel's smile was getting tired by the time Greg finished taking pictures, and her stomach was growling.

"That's about two hundred," Greg said. "Thank goodness for digital cameras. There should be a good one or two for you to use."

"How much for a copy of every one of them?" Clancy asked.

"I'll make you a good deal," Greg said as he packed up his equipment.

"Why would you want all of them?" Angel asked.

"Because you're in them," Clancy answered and kissed her on the cheek. "We'll talk about the pictures later. Right now, let's go eat."

Angel nodded. "I can sure agree with that."

Angel piled food on her plate and carried it over to a table. "I could eat a whole cow if someone would knock the horns off and heat it up on a charcoal grill. Who would have thought that church and posing for pictures could take so much energy?"

"Add in what we did half the night, and it's a wonder we have enough energy to blink our eyes," Clancy teased.

"That would be Angela Conrad," a lady whispered from the next table over. "Meredith told me she was Clancy's high school sweetheart before he started dating Melissa."

"Well, when he gets tired of her, he can send her over my way," one of the older men at that table said with a chuckle.

"Oh, Raymond, you're too damned old to know what to do with her." The man beside him punched him playfully on the arm. "Besides, what would someone that pretty want with an old coot like you? I heard tell she's got an oil company and enough money to buy this whole town and plow it under for a garden if she wanted to."

"Gossip, gossip." Clancy grinned.

"But it's nice gossip, and as long as they're talking about us, someone else is getting a rest. That's what my granny used to say." Angel picked up a napkin and spread it out over her lap, then reached across the table for another one to set beside her plate. "I'm messy when I eat ribs, but I love them!"

"Seems to me you like food, period," Clancy said. "And I do love a woman who isn't picky about what they eat."

"You would, too, if you'd lived for a whole year on pork and beans and wienies," she said. "Besides, I'm one of those fortunate women who can eat whatever she wants and not worry about calories or fat grams. I'm so active and burn them so fast that I can eat what I want."

"Just another thing that I love about you." Clancy picked up a rib with his fingers.

"Let me have your attention." Tom tapped the edge of his glass with his fork. "The caterers are bringing a little champagne toast around to your tables now," he said as waitresses brought silver trays with fluted crystal glasses of champagne and set one beside each person.

Tom raised his own glass high in the hot afternoon breeze. "I would like to propose a toast to my new bride. To my Merrie, who has made me happy at a time in my life when I thought happiness was just a dream I had lost forever. May we celebrate our fiftieth anniversary together," Tom winked at Meredith and clinked his glass against hers. "I love you, darlin'."

Everyone took a sip, and then Tom raised his glass again. "I've got another toast," he said. "This is to Clancy and his Angel. They were high school sweethearts, and now they're back together again. To you two kids. May you find the same happiness Merrie and I have found." He raised his glass high toward them and then polished off the rest of what was in it.

"Thank you." Clancy rose to his feet. "And a toast from me if anyone has anything left in their glasses. If not, raise your hand, and the caterers will be around to fill it again. To my mama, who's been my friend as well as my parent. I thought my father was the most wonderful man in the whole world, and I have to admit, I didn't think I'd ever like anyone else taking his place. But Tom has made a place of his own, both in Mama's heart and in mine. So, to Tom, my new friend. And to Angel—my one and only." Clancy clinked his glass with Angel's and tossed back the rest of his champagne in one swallow.

He had barely sat back down when one of the caterers brought him a cordless phone. "For you, sir. The phone rang in the kitchen area, and one of my helpers answered it. The caller asked for you."

"Hello?" Clancy pushed the button and waited.

His eyes suddenly filled with tears and his chin quivered. Angel looped her arm in his. "Is everything all right?"

He shook his head. "We'll be there as soon as we can get there," he said. "Angel is right here beside me. I'll bring her with me. Tell him we're on our way."

"What's wrong?" Angel asked.

"That was Anna. Red's had a heart attack. They've got him in the hospital in Denison, and he's asking for the two of us. I was wondering why they weren't here. Mama would have invited them for sure."

Tears ran down Angel's cheeks, dripping off her jaw. "I'll get my things together."

"Here, take this." Clancy pressed a white hanky into her hands. "I'll tell Mama and Tom and be right behind you."

Chapter 15

RED'S WIFE, ANNA, MET THEM AT THE HOSPITAL DOOR. HER makeup was smeared from all the tears she had cried. Her trademark skintight jeans had long since lost their perfect crease from top to bottom.

"How is he?" Angel hugged her old friend tightly and felt Anna's thin shoulders shudder as she gave way to a whole new set of sobs.

"Red's goin' to make it. The doctor's said this heart attack was just a little one, but it sure scared me. While we were waiting for the ambulance, I realized that I didn't even know how much I loved him until I nearly lost him. I thought he was gone, Angel. I really thought he was gone." She wept even harder. "Oh, Clancy." Anna broke one arm away and brought him into a three-way hug. "He started asking for you a couple of hours ago. I told him to wait until we saw the doctor, but Red said to call you right now. Only immediate family is allowed in intensive care, but he's pitched such a fit, they said you two could go in if it will calm him down."

"Are you sure?" Angel drew back and looked at her. "We don't want to upset or worry him. Most of all, we don't want to excite him. Maybe we ought to wait till tomorrow morning."

"Nope. Red intends to see Clancy tonight," Anna said. "I'll go with you up to the floor where he is and wait in the lobby until he visits with you. The nurses sure wouldn't allow all three of us in there at once. They said you could only stay five minutes. He's done told me what he intends to say, and I agree with him, Clancy. So, listen to him. And besides, he's afraid to go to sleep before he speaks his mind."

They found Red in a room at the end of the intensive care ward. An oxygen tube was stretched around his freckled face and attached under his nose. An IV dripped into his sinewy left arm, which had seen more hard work in its sixty years than most men could experience in two or three lifetimes. He looked so much smaller in a hospital bed than he did when Angel had wheeled and dealed with him over oil wells. When he sat across a conference table from her, haggling over the price of a well, he seemed to be ten feet tall and made of steel. Tonight, he looked like someone's grandpa, with wispy red hair turning gray and deep wrinkles around his mouth.

"Afternoon, you two kids." Red smiled and a bit of color returned to his face. "Glad you are here. Saves me a trip up to your place, because I was determined to see you even if I had to crawl out of the bed and check myself out of this place."

"Red, you old devil." Clancy bent over the bed and hugged him. "You've given us a scare. Angel cried all the way down here, and I couldn't swallow the lump in my throat."

Angel had to tiptoe and then bend over to kiss him on the forehead. "The trip seemed like it took two days instead of a little over an hour."

"I'm glad y'all love me that much," Red said. "It'll make what I've got to say a lot easier. Now I've been asking—even begging—you to come to work for me, Clancy. You've always been like a son to me and Anna, the son we couldn't have."

Red paused and took a deep breath. "Not that you've been around much lately. But you're a grown man with your own life to live, and I know you have liked teaching high school kids. I'm too old for the stress of running an oil company. I've got to slow down. I don't just want you to work for me. I need you to help me."

"All right." Clancy nodded. "I was going to call you next week with my decision anyway—"

Red held up a hand. "Now hear me out. I'm talking about more than just a job. I figure I've got a few years left, and anything I can't teach you, Angel can. She's smarter'n me, anyway, but I'm older and I've got more experience, so you're goin' to learn from me first. Me and Anna had our wills drawn up a while back, and Texanna Red will be yours when I'm gone. All of it, lock, stock, rigs, and barrel. And the time has come for you to start learnin' how to run it. You're throwing away that degree in geology and chemistry, as far as I'm concerned."

"Red, I can't let you do that, not when you've had a scare like this," Clancy said.

"Hush, and let me finish. Patty told me last week about you two. You and Angel can be competitors, or you can be partners. I don't give a damn if later on down the road you consolidate Texanna Red and Conrad Oil, or if you keep them separate and fight over who makes the most money. I want you to know how to run the company so I won't cash in my chips worryin' about some smart woman like Angel takin' advantage of your lack of knowledge. I'd like to see my two favorite people together before I die." He closed his eyes and took another deep breath.

"Red, I'll work for you, but you don't have to leave the oil company to me," Clancy assured him.

"It's already done. Now, get on out of here," Red whispered dramatically. "Come see me tomorrow. First, I have to teach you to run it. Half of the company is yours right now, the rest when I'm gone. Maybe before that day, I'll get to bounce a grandbaby on my shaky old knees?"

Angel suppressed a chuckle. "Red, you connivin' old cuss, you're not about to run my life, even if you did have a heart attack. You might have grandchildren someday, but it won't be because you pretended to be sicker than you really were. You're tougher than shoe leather and buzzard bait combined. I'm goin' home, and when we get back tomorrow, you better be sittin' up in bed, unwired from all these contraptions, and makin' oil deals on the phone. Good night, you old sweetheart." She kissed him on the cheek and headed out the door, then turned around to wait on Clancy.

Red opened one eye. "I'm not one bit tougher than you are, smarty pants. And, Clancy, I'm holdin' you to your word. Call that school and tell them you're resignin' before school starts up, and be ready to go to work in your new office on Wednesday. That'll give you two days to find a place and get moved down here to Denison. I just signed a deal on a new building. Now go catch that girl and make her your bride before she gets away."

"It's not that easy, Red." Clancy winked at Angel. "I'm not entirely sure she wants to be caught."

"Then you'd better hurry up, Son. She's gettin' away." Red talked out of the side of his mouth and closed his eyes again.

Clancy crossed the room and took Angel's hand in his. "I wouldn't want you to get away."

"I'm not going anywhere." Angel sighed. "I really was afraid he'd be gone by the time we got here," she said as the two of them made their way down the hall to the waiting room.

"Me too." Clancy swung open the door.

Anna stood up and dabbed at her eyes with a tissue. "Did he talk to you?"

"I start at Texanna on Wednesday morning. If I've got a question, and I'm sure I will have many as I learn the business, I'll just call Angel."

"Thank the Lord." Anna shuddered. "I've been around the oil business all our married life. More than forty years, but I don't know jack squat about any of it. I can throw a party, flutter my eyes, and help talk a deal, but if I had to fill out a single form, I'd probably be signin' the whole business over to a swindler. I'm glad you'll be there, Clancy."

He took a step back. "Is the new office very far from Conrad Oil?"

"A block down and across the street. We bought the old bank building. His staff is in there right now moving all our stuff in."

"I know exactly where that is. I'll show you." Angel let go of his hand and wrapped Anna up in her arms before stepping back. "I'm so relieved. I'm going back in there with him now, but neither of you can know what a burden you've taken off my shoulders."

"We'll be going. If you need us for anything," Clancy said, "just call, and we'll be here as soon as we can. If we don't hear from you, we'll be back in the morning. How long do you think they'll keep him?"

"Couple of days, the doctor says—if Red promises not to go to work for two weeks when he gets out. And don't forget to call your mother and tell her Red's okay. Today was a special day for her and Tom. I'm so sorry we interrupted it."

"No problem," Clancy said.

"If you need a place to stay or to freshen up, my apartment is just minutes from here," Angel said.

"I'm not leaving his side." Anna hurried out of the room.

"I want what they've got," Clancy said when she was gone.

Angel sighed. "Me too."

———————————

"Welcome to my city home." Angel opened the front door when they arrived at her apartment and stepped inside. She flipped the light switch and motioned toward the dining room. "Just set those groceries on the table." Then she pulled the drapes to let in light through the balcony doors.

Clancy put the bags down just as rain began to beat against the doors. "Looks like rain follows us wherever we go." He walked up behind her and circled her waist with his arms.

"Sure looks that way." Angel covered his hands with hers. "It's just rain. I command that cloud, if it's planning to produce a tornado, to go tear up something a hundred miles away from me and you." She waved her hand toward the dark masses.

"If I were those clouds, I wouldn't test you." He grinned.

She turned around and slipped her arms around his neck. "I was so scared, Clancy, and now that we know Red is all right…"

"I know." He pulled her closer to his chest. "Seems like we've faced enough storms for a lifetime, but you know what they say... What doesn't kill us makes us stronger.."

"If that's the truth, we should be able to bench press an Angus bull." She laid her head on his chest and listened to the steady beat of his heart.

"We've got a lot to do in the next few days. I need to call my boss and turn in my resignation, find an apartment, and..."

"You don't need an apartment. You can stay with me," Angel said. "I'm goin' back to Conrad Oil tomorrow morning for some peace and quiet. We'll both be busy, and I want to see you whenever I can, so living here with me seems to be the answer."

"Thank you, Angel," he whispered into her ear.

"We'll see how we get along when we have to work and come home cranky," she said. "Which reminds me. I get cranky when I'm hungry, and neither of us got more than a couple bites of food down before we got the call, so are we going to order out or cook?"

"You said you don't cook." He began to massage the knots from her back.

"I can make a mean ham sandwich, and I know how to

heat up a can of bean with bacon soup to go with it, but if you want cooked food, you'll have to do it." She turned and laid her face on his chest.

"I can cook, but it's not gourmet," he admitted.

"Then tomorrow night, when we're sure that Red is completely out of the woods, we'll go to the farm and Hilda will feed us. When she sees how happy I am, maybe she won't put rat poison in your potatoes. You've got two hours to stop that wonderful massaging on my back." She wiggled in appreciation.

"We would really be starved in two hours if I keep this up, because it would lead to the bedroom," he said. "If you'll make the entree of ham à la sandwich, I'll make the side dish of soup à la bean with bacon."

"Deal." Angel reached into the first grocery bag and pulled out a loaf of whole grain bread and a package of ham. "Let the gourmet cookin' begin."

"Why in the world do you live in two places?" Clancy opened the can of soup and rummaged around in the cabinets until he found a saucepan.

"Because I wanted two places. Sometimes I didn't feel like driving to the farm when we got home from a gig. Sometimes one of the girls needed a place to sleep if they didn't want to go home. So, I bought this apartment for those times."

"It's a lovely place, Angel." He scanned the apartment. "But I'm surprised you don't have a porch swing here."

"I've got one ordered. I had to have it custom made to fit on the balcony," she admitted.

"Angel, what are we going to do about us?" Clancy asked as he heated the soup.

"What about us?" she asked. "We'll both work. We'll come home either here or the farm. Red's office staff will take you under their wings and smother you half to death. Those women have been with him since I've known him. Some of them are probably the same people you used to visit when you and your daddy came down here on Saturdays. The geologist and the lawyer are pretty new, but they're friendly. You'll like them. In a couple of weeks, you'll fit right in. Don't worry. You're smart, and you'll learn fast." She finished making two sandwiches and carried them to the kitchen table.

"We need to talk about *us*," he said.

"I'm in love with you, Clancy Morgan. I loved you from the first day of kindergarten." She stopped to kiss him on the cheek as she passed by the stove.

"I wanted to court you like a lady. I wanted to take you everywhere I didn't take you all those years ago, and then when you had fallen in love with me, I wanted to ask you to marry me." Clancy turned to face her. "You deserve all that and more."

"But what I want is just you," she told him. "I want to feel you near me, even when we're too tired for sex. I want to fall asleep in your arms and wake up to find you beside me, but before I do it, I want to hear you say—"

"I love you, Angel. I've loved you for ten years." Clancy's next kisses were long, lingering, and steamy hot.

"We might fight," she purred.

"We'll make up," he said.

"We might disagree. I'm obnoxious when I argue," Angel said.

"So am I, but we'll work that out when the day comes." Clancy smiled.

"I like the way you think." She pulled his lips down to hers for another long kiss.

Chapter 16

"Mornin', Angel," Patty greeted her with a big, innocent smile.

"Call them all in," Angel said. "Just us girls, in the conference room in three minutes, pronto."

The grin faded from Patty's face in an instant. She pushed the red button on the intercom sitting on her desk and said, "Angel's home, ladies. She says meet in three minutes in the conference room, and I think we're in trouble."

Angel walked over to the window and looked down at the main street while she waited for her friends to assemble behind her. She wanted them to think she was so angry she didn't want to face them, but it was hard to keep a smile off her face. Especially when she thought about Red in his hospital bed trying to act sicker than he really was, and when she thought about waking up beside Clancy that morning.

Patty cleared her throat, and Angel turned around to find all five sitting in their places around the conference table. "I ought to shoot every one of you for the stunt you pulled, but your intuition was better than mine. I have to thank you."

Patty wiped her brow with the back of her hand in a dramatic gesture.

Mindy sighed.

Allie rolled her eyes to the ceiling, and Susan giggled.

"Want to tell us about it?" Bonnie asked.

"Nope." Angel shook her head. "After what you did, not one of you deserves to hear the details. But Clancy and I intend to put the past behind us and get on with the future. I finally have closure," she managed to say and hoped her expression didn't give anything away. "Susan, bring me up to date on what's going on in the front office. The rest of you can meet with me at thirty-minute intervals—"

"Hey…" Bonnie stopped her midsentence. "We're your friends. We've shared everything from busted fingernails to divorces. We only did this to help you get over the sorry sucker who made you walk around here all down in the mouth."

"I'm over the past. I told you that." Then she started to laugh.

One minute everything was as quiet as a prelude to a

funeral, the next minute Angel was wiping tears from her face and hiccuping. "You are all a bunch of devils, and I love every one of you—horns, pointy little tails, and all." She pulled a tissue from a box in the middle of the table. "Clancy is moving in with me. We're goin' to make it this time! I've realized anything worth having is worth fightin' for, and no one is getting between me and Clancy Morgan again. Maybe I should have fought for him all those years ago, but then if I had, we wouldn't be where we are today. Clancy and I needed ten years to grow up enough to realize what we have, and I thank all of you for seeing that when I was blind."

"Hot damn," Patty swore loudly. "Is there goin' to be a weddin'?"

"Maybe someday." Angel nodded.

"Someday..." Allie drew out the word and raised an eyebrow.

"Let's get back to business," Angel said. "And you should know that Red has hired a new man who's pretty sharp. His name just happens to be Clancy Morgan, and I don't think even *I* will be able to blink my pretty lashes and get him to give me a good deal."

"Well, isn't it a small world," Mindy said. "Angel, it

might take a while for us to forgive that man, but we promise to give him a chance. Right, girls?"

"Right," they chorused.

"Now, let's get back to work. I'll be in when you and Susan get done." Mindy headed for the door.

"Nothing much has happened since you've been away," Susan said when she and Angel were alone. "Except for Red's heart attack. Shook us all up. We reckoned he'd be around until eternity." She toyed with a lock of her hair. "Life sure don't offer any guarantees, does it, Angel? I'm goin' to tell Richie to set the date. Maybe a Thanksgiving wedding would be good. Bonnie will be married by then. I want us to fly to Jamaica and tie the knot down there."

"If that's what you want, then go after it." Angel led the way from the conference room to her office and sat down behind her desk. "I'm hoping that Clancy and I will just wake up some morning and know that it's the day and find us a judge."

"I'm really happy for you," Susan said. "Guess he turned out better than we expected. We shouldn't punish him forever for a mistake he made ten years ago, but if I'm honest, it might take me a while to get over still wanting to shoot him."

"I understand." Angel opened a portfolio on her desk and

reviewed Susan's proposition for a new advertising campaign. "Looks really good," she muttered, turning the pages. "Let me know when you're ready to spring it on the oil industry."

"Will do, and it's good to have you home. Gotta run. Never know what might come walkin' in the front door." Susan stood up.

Angel had barely gotten through her mini-meetings with each of her friends when Patty buzzed to tell her Clancy was on the phone.

"I need a refresher course," he moaned. "They're talking drillers and roughnecks and rigs and casings, and I'm having trouble keeping up."

"You'll learn. Old dogs can be retaught if they want to learn," she said. "Remember, anything worth having is worth fighting for. Like Red told you last night, half of Texanna Red is yours right now. If you want to keep it, you'll learn."

"How can I learn this and court you too? I can't think about business for thinking about you," he said.

"Then you better learn to control your thoughts a little better. From nine to five only think about Texanna Red, and from then on you belong to me." Angel laughed.

"Are we still going to the farm tonight? Are we going down that curvy back road?" he asked.

"Clancy, it's twice as far to go the highway, and it only takes thirty seconds to cross the bridge over into Hendrix. You should have had to cross the old bridge. It looked and felt like it might collapse anytime. The new one is concrete and sturdy," she said.

She couldn't imagine anyone being so afraid of heights. How in the world was he ever going to put on a hard hat and climb to the top of a rig for an inspection?

"Are we fighting?" he asked just as shortly.

"Who knows?" she said. "But we'll talk about it later. I've got a meeting with Margie this afternoon, and I'd rather do battle with the Hendrix bridge any day than that old barracuda. You better hope Red is up and well by the time she knows you're a new person in the office. She'll eat you for lunch and lick her fingers afterward."

"You think I can't hold my own with her?" Clancy's voice held a challenging edge.

"Not if you don't learn the difference between a rig and a casing," she threw right back at him.

"I'll see you at five. And *I'll* drive. We'll take my Bronco," he said.

"Anything you say, sweetheart. Have a good day," she said.

She was still thinking about work when she got home that evening. Clancy's Bronco sat in the driveway beside her parking place. She opened the door and found his bags packed beside it, but he was sleeping soundly on the couch. She sat down on the floor beside him and stared at him for ten minutes, trying to figure out what she should do. If he was her competitor forever, would it cause trouble between them?

That old familiar feeling tickled the inside of her mind, and Angel knew without another thought what she was going to do. Clancy was going to face some difficult times as he learned a new business and had to face more responsibility than he'd ever had before. She'd be there for him, and if they fought along the way, then they could damn well make up afterward, because she was committing herself for the long haul right now.

She leaned over and kissed him on the cheek. "Hey, sleepyhead, we've got to go see Red, and I called Hilda. Supper will be on the table at seven, so you'd better wake up."

He didn't open his eyes, but he did smile. "You know how afraid I am of heights. Always have been. Couldn't even dive off the dam in Tishomingo because it looked like it was six miles to the bottom."

"I know." She kissed his eyelids and his cheeks, rough

with a five-o'clock beard. And then his mouth. "But you'll get over it."

━━━━━━━━━

They found Red sitting up in bed with a cell phone and a yellow legal pad in front of him. Anna's jeans were creased perfectly, and she'd visited the hairdresser that day.

"Hey, how'd the first day go? Dennis, the geologist, said you were frustrated but determined." Red smiled at them. "By the way, I want the offshore drillers to start spending three weeks out and three weeks in. Give them more time at home with their families at a stretch."

"He's back to wheelin' and dealin'," Anna groaned. "He's being released today, and the doctor says he can work from home, but only for half a day this week. Doc says it'll be two weeks before he can go all day. You'll do fine, Clancy. In a while, you'll know as much about it as us old dogs. You young'uns learn fast."

"Now, talk to me about you two," Red said, setting his legal pad and cell phone aside. "I want to know why neither of you ever mentioned the other's name in all these years."

"Wasn't any reason," Clancy said. "I didn't know Angel

was in the oil business, and I figured she was married to someone else."

"I thought he and Melissa were married and living happily ever after, amen," Angel said. "And my intuition didn't tell me different."

Red chuckled. "Must be the only time it's failed you. I'd still pay you big bucks to sit behind a desk and tell me when that crazy feeling hits you. Clancy, if you don't take advantage of this girl's sixth sense, you're a lunatic."

"Yes, sir." Clancy nodded. "And I'll sure be glad when you're back on the job to answer all my questions, because she's the competition, and she's pretty closemouthed when it comes to information I could use." He shot a slow wink over at Angel.

"Good for you." Red looked at Angel with pride. "Keep him on his toes and make him work for what he wants. In the business *and* in the bedroom."

"Red!" Angel blushed.

"Get on out of here." The older man waved them away. "I've got a decision or two to make, and I don't have your smarty pants instincts. I have to think about things," he told her. "Let me know when you decide to tie the knot. I've got a great honeymoon in mind. Hell, me and Anna just might go with you."

"No, we will not!" Anna exclaimed. "The doctor said no honeymoon activities for a while."

"See you." Angel kissed Red on the forehead. "But when and if Clancy and I decide to waste time and money on a honeymoon, we'll go alone."

"If you two are even thinking about a honeymoon, just remember that the wedding has to come first." Red tucked his chin in and studied her over the top of his gold-rimmed glasses.

"I know that." She met his gaze.

"Well, damn it all, Anna. She ain't softened up one bit with someone to love her, after all." Red grinned. "See you at work tomorrow, Clancy."

—————

They left town in the Bronco, Clancy behind the wheel, his knuckles getting whiter as they got closer to the Hendrix Bridge. His jaw was set in determination and he turned on the radio to distract himself, but he didn't talk to her. He would drive fifty extra miles a day not to have to look that far down at the Red River flowing under the bridge, but if she wanted to go this way, then by damn, this was the way they would go.

"Clancy, turn this car around and go the other way," Angel said when they were about a mile from the bridge. "Or else move over and let me drive."

"Hell no!" he practically shouted. "I'm driving, and I'm driving across that bridge. A smart lady told me one time that I need to face my fears."

"Like I told you before, the old one was a lot scarier than this one," she told him.

"If that was the case, then I definitely would have let you drive and would have closed my eyes the whole way across it."

His heart did double time when he saw the bridge ahead. Two kids riding bicycles were crossing, coming toward them, so he had to slow down. He gripped the steering wheel as tightly as he had the first time his father had let him drive at the age of eleven, and took a deep breath. When they were right in the middle of the bridge, he stopped the vehicle.

"Come here," Clancy said. Angel popped the console up and moved over next to him.

"I need to feel you next to me, Angel. I've been thinking ever since we left the hospital. I'm scared of this new change, and I'm damned scared of this stupid bridge. But I can overcome anything with you beside me."

"That's right, Clancy, you can." Angel snuggled against him. "We've crossed worse bridges than that one back there, you know. In the past month, we've crossed a lot of bridges. I've met you in the middle of some of them, and you've had to meet me in the middle of some that were higher than this. We can make it together, honey. Let's go home."

"Before we do, I want to ask you right here on top of this hellacious bridge if you'll marry me, Angel. I still don't deserve you after what I did all those years ago, but I'm hopelessly in love with you." He kissed her and forgot about where they were.

"Okay," she said. "Whenever and wherever you say. When you're ready, call the tune, and I'll dance to it. But, darlin', there's a police car pulling in behind us with the lights flashing."

The policeman got out of the car and walked up to the door. "Y'all havin' car trouble?" he asked. "Oh, I see that it's you, Miz Angela. Are you all right?"

"I'm great," she said.

"She said she'd marry me!" Clancy told the policeman. "I just proposed and she said yes."

"I could think of more romantic places than this"—the policeman grinned—"but congratulations!"

Hilda opened the farmhouse door for them with a frown on her face.

"I'm engaged!" Angel said.

"Well, hot damn! It's about time both of you woke up." Hilda's frown turned into a wide smile, and she rushed over to hug Angel. "I was just about to leave. Supper is on the stove. Does Jimmy know yet? Can I tell him when he gets to work tomorrow?"

"Of course you can," Angel said.

"Just stack the dishes on the counter when you're finished." Hilda removed her apron and hung it on the back of a bench in the foyer. "I'll put them in the dishwasher tomorrow morning, but I won't be here until after you leave for work. My great-granddaughter has a dance recital tomorrow, and I promised her I'd be there." She stopped and pointed her finger at Clancy's nose. "If you ever make Angel cry again, you'll have to deal with me. And when I finish, the buzzards get the leftovers. Now have a good supper."

"Whew!" Clancy wiped sweat from his forehead. "Did I pass inspection at last? I can't tell by the way she talks."

"Yes, of course." Angel smiled. "Now, will you hold me one more time and tell me what you said on that bridge? That you're not scared when I'm with you. Was I dreaming or did you propose?"

He dropped down on one knee and took her hand in his. "I'll do it right this time. Will you marry me, Angel, next Friday night?"

"Yes, Clancy, I'll marry you, but why next Friday night?" she asked.

"You'll see." He stood up and gathered her into his arms for a kiss that sealed their promises and their hearts together forever and ever.

Epilogue

"WHAT AM I DOING?" ANGEL LOOKED IN THE MIRROR THE very next Friday night. The same woman with the same kinky hair that she saw every morning looked back at her, but she didn't have the answers to the questions in Angel's heart. "Well, it's time," she said to her reflection. "Feels kind of crazy, but hey, I said whenever and wherever. If this is what Clancy wants, I'm willing to do it."

Angela got into her shiny Jaguar and drove down Main Street in Tishomingo. The city rolled up the sidewalks at five o'clock and only one red light worked after ten, even if it was Friday night. She passed a few cars full of kids out for a drive, but mostly the little town was quiet. She made a sharp right turn across the Pennington Creek Bridge and carefully drove her car to the sandbar where a few people waited in folding chairs.

Red met her at the car. He wore his best western-cut suit with a carnation on the lapel. "You're beautiful, and I'm glad for this honor." He tucked her arm into his.

Fiddle music began off to one side. Then she heard Mindy on the keyboard, playing a few soft chords. Clancy had said there would be a few people and the girls, but that their wedding would be small, and now the band was set up to one side, playing as Red led her down the aisle between the two rows of chairs.

"Who gives this woman to be married to this man?" Dillon asked, but his voice didn't boom like it did in the church.

"Her friends and I do," Red said as he handed Angel's hand to Clancy.

Dillon continued. "We are gathered here because this is the time of night that Clancy first met Angel, and this is the time of night, I'm told, that they parted company exactly ten years ago this day. Clancy says this is what he should have done that night. And now we're doing something not everyone gets to do in their lifetime. We're getting to go back in time."

"Angel, I've got something to tell you," Clancy said loud and clear. "I remember the words I spoke to you ten years ago, and I'm sorry, but like you've said, we are stronger now, and I for one am glad for this second chance."

Angel reached out and took his hands in hers. She had chosen her dream wedding dress, white satin with a short train. Instead of a veil, she wore white baby roses braided into a crown on top of her unruly hair that she'd worn down just for Clancy. "I've got something to tell you, Clancy," Angel said. "I'm glad that Fate, or Destiny, or God—whoever or whatever—has given us a second chance, and I do not intend to waste a moment of it."

Clancy looked down into her eyes, and suddenly, Angel felt as if they were alone on the creek bank, just like they had been ten years ago.

He cleared his throat and said, "I love you with my whole heart, Angel. It's been branded with your name for the past ten years, and I want to stay with you forever, through this lifetime and eternity."

Angel noticed that her friends were brushing away tears, and she had to swallow the lump in her throat before she could say anything.

"Clancy, I took one look at you when we were still in kindergarten, and I wanted to stay with you forever. And now I will, through this lifetime and eternity too."

The minister spoke again.

"Angela Conrad and Clancy Morgan have made their

vows. These solemn promises are binding in the sight of God and these witnesses, and we come to the giving and receiving of rings," he said and went on with the traditional ceremony, up to and including a very passionate kiss.

"And now I've got something to do," Clancy said.

Dillon handed him a stick.

Clancy drew two entwining hearts in the sand and wrote *FOREVER* in the space where they connected. "I love you, Angel."

Tears hung on her heavy dark lashes when she said, "I love you, Clancy."

"Now, let's go out to my house and have a little reception. I've invited a few friends for cake and champagne," Meredith said.

Angel giggled. "That means the whole town."

She gathered up the tail of her white satin wedding dress but hadn't even taken one step when Clancy scooped her up and carried her to her car. "I hope you don't mind if I drive this thing."

"Do you know how to drive a stick shift?" she asked.

"Honey, I can drive anything that's got a steering wheel, and with you beside me, I could even drive it over a high bridge," he said.

"With you beside me, I could ride with you over those high spots." She smiled. "Let's get this reception done with and go home to the farm. We've got a three-day weekend to enjoy our honeymoon."

─────────

Later that night, in the privacy of their bedroom at the farmhouse, they ate the cheese and fruit left by Hilda and tasted the sweetness of a bottle of champagne that Tom handed them when they drove away from Tishomingo. Then Clancy undressed her slowly in the moonlight and carried her to the bed, where he gently laid her down.

"I love you, Mrs. Morgan, and I hope we have a dozen children," he whispered into her ear.

"I love you, too, Clancy. There's no time like right now to get started on that big family, now, is there?"

Love sultry, small-town romance?
You're in for a real treat! Read on for a look
at the first book in the
Welcome to Magnolia Bay series
from Babette de Jongh.

Chapter 1

"I HATE PEOPLE." ABBY CURTIS WADDED UP THE HEM OF her yellow bathrobe and dropped to her knees in the ditch. A pair of green eyes stared at her from the middle of the culvert. "Here, kitty, kitty," she called.

The eyes blinked, but the kitten stayed put. Another stray dumped in front of Aunt Reva's house, and it wasn't going to trust humans again anytime soon. For a nanosecond, Abby thought about running back to the house to get Reva, but something told her the kitten would skedaddle the moment Abby turned her back.

Reva's dog, Georgia, a Jack Russell terrier/cattle dog mix, peered through the other side of the culvert and whined. The kitten spun around to face the dog and hissed.

"Georgia." Abby snapped her fingers. "Stay."

The frightened kitten puffed up and growled at Georgia. Abby didn't have Reva's way with animals. But with the little dog's expert help, she might be able to catch the kitten without bothering her aunt, who was in the house packing for a long-postponed trip.

Georgia whined again and the kitten backed up farther, her full attention on the dog.

Thankful the ditch had been mowed and recently treated for fire ants, Abby eased forward onto her belly in the damp grass. She reached into the culvert, ignoring the cool, muddy water that seeped through her robe and soaked her T-shirt and panties. Shutting out images of snakes and spiders, she scooted closer and stretched out farther.

Just a little bit more…

Georgia seemed to know exactly what to do. She fake-lunged toward the kitten, who spat and hopped backward into Abby's outstretched hand. "Gotcha!" Abby grabbed the kitten's scruff.

The kitten whirled and spun and scratched, but Abby held on, even when it sank needlelike teeth into Abby's hand.

"Shh. Shh." Abby got to her knees and stroked the kitten's dark tortoiseshell fur. A girl, then. Like calicos, tortoiseshell cats were almost always female. "You're okay, little girl. You're all right."

Abby's robe had come open in the front, and the kitten pedaled all four feet with claws extended, scratching gouges in Abby's exposed skin. She held on to the scruff of the kitten's neck, crooning and humming. "You're okay, baby."

Georgia leaped with excitement, begging to see the kitten, who continued to struggle and scratch and bite.

"No, Georgia." Abby wrapped the kitten in the folds of her robe and held it close. It calmed, but Abby could feel its body heaving with every desperate breath. "Not yet. She's too scared."

If this catch didn't stick, Abby wouldn't get another chance. Her fingers touched a raw, bloody patch on the kitten's back: road rash from being thrown out of a moving vehicle.

God, Abby hated people. No wonder Aunt Reva had all but turned into a hermit, living out here in the boondocks alongside the kind of people who would do this. But then, Abby had learned that evil lived everywhere—north and south, city and country. She cuddled the kitten close, even while it tried to flay her skin with its desperate claws.

"Nobody's going to hurt you, I promise. Nobody's going to hurt you, not ever again." She could make that promise, because she knew Reva would keep the kitten or find it an even better home. All strays were welcome at Bayside Barn.

Abby herself was proof of that.

Disgusted with all of humanity, Abby struggled up out of the ditch, her mud-caked barn boots slipping on the dew-wet grass. She had just scrambled onto solid ground when a Harley blasted past, turned in at the drive next door, and stopped just past the ditch.

Uncomfortably aware that her bathrobe gaped open indecently and her hair hadn't seen a hairbrush since yesterday afternoon, Abby hid behind the tall hedge between Aunt Reva's place and the abandoned estate next door. Georgia clawed Abby's legs in a "Help, pick me up" gesture.

"Lord, Georgia, I can't hold both of you."

Determined, Georgia scrabbled at Abby's legs. One-handed, Abby scooped up all thirty pounds of the scaredy-cat dog. "It's only a motorcycle."

The sound of garbage trucks in the distance promised an even more terrifying situation if she didn't get the kitten into the house soon. She held Georgia in one hand and clutched the covered-up kitten with the other, jiggling both of them in a hopefully soothing motion. "You're okay. You're both okay."

The loud motorbike idled near the estate's rusted-out mailbox. The rider put both booted feet down on the gravel drive. Tall, broad-shouldered, he wore motorcycle leathers and a black helmet with a tinted visor.

Georgia licked Abby's chin, a plea to hurry back to the house before the garbage trucks ravaging the next block over ushered in the apocalypse.

"Shh. I want to go home, too, but..." If she fled from her hiding place, the motorcycle dude would notice a flash of movement when Abby's yellow robe flapped behind her like a flag. What was this guy doing before 8:00 a.m. parking his motorcycle in a lonely driveway on this dead-end country road?

The rider got off the motorcycle and removed his helmet. His light-brown hair stood on end, then feathered down to cover his jacket collar.

His hair was the only soft thing about him. From his tanned skin to his angular face to his rigid jaw, from his wide shoulders to his bulging thighs to his scuffed black boots, the guy looked hard.

He waded through the tall weeds to the center of the easement and pulled up the moldy *For Sale* sign that had stood there for years. He tossed the sign into the weed-filled ditch and stalked back to his motorcycle. The beast roared down the potholed driveway to the old abandoned house, scattering gravel.

Quinn Lockhart sped down the long drive, a list of obstacles spinning through his head:

1. Cracked brick facade: Possible foundation problems.
2. Swimming pool: Green with algae and full of tadpoles, frogs—probably snakes too.
3. Overgrown acreage: Ten acres of out-of-control shrubs choked with vines and weeds.

He'd seen all this on his first and only inspection; he knew what he was getting into. Though he had never attempted to renovate and flip a long-abandoned house before, he knew he possessed the necessary skills to do it successfully. Hell. Even JP—the ex-business-partner and ex-friend he'd known since high school—had made a fricking fortune flipping houses. If all-talk, no-action JP could do it, Quinn could roll up his sleeves and do it ten times better. The sale of this polished-up diamond would provide the seed money he needed to start his own construction business in Magnolia Bay and, maybe even more important, prove his talent to future clients.

When his lowball offer was accepted, he hadn't known whether to whoop or moan. The hidden gem of this dilapidated estate could only go up in value. Located on a remote back road several miles outside Magnolia Bay and an easy hour to New Orleans, the place was a rare find he wouldn't have known about if he hadn't been dating the local real estate agent who helped him find an apartment here after his divorce. But the next-to-nothing price and a small stash of cash for renovations had consumed every penny of the equity he'd received in the divorce. And he still hadn't quite convinced himself that leaving New Orleans to follow his ex and their son to her hometown was the best decision he'd ever made.

He reminded himself that moving to Magnolia Bay was the only way he could spend enough time with his teenage son. After years of working more than he should and leaving Sean's raising to Melissa, Quinn knew this was his last chance to rebuild the relationship between him and his son. Quinn was hoping they'd bond over the renovation, if he could convince Sean that helping out would be fun. So it wasn't just a business decision; it was a last-ditch effort to be the kind of father Sean deserved.

When Delia Simmons, his real estate agent, showed him this estate, a thrill of excitement and hope had skittered through him. This old place had good bones. Putting it back together would be the first step toward putting his life back together.

And when she told him the rumor she'd heard around town that the adjacent acreage between this road and the bay might soon become available as well... Maybe it wasn't a sign from God, exactly, but it sure lit a fire under his butt. With the right timing, he could use the money from the sale of this place to buy the strip of Magnolia Bay waterfront land that ran behind all five estates on this dead-end road.

He could subdivide the bayside marshland along the existing estates' property lines, then sell each parcel to its adjoining estate. If he had enough money, he could build nice elevated walkways from each estate to the marsh-edged bay, maybe even haul in enough sand to make a community beach complete with boat docks and shaded pavilions.

Maybe he was dreaming too big. But he couldn't stop thinking that with perfect timing on the sale of the estate and the availability of the waterfront land, he could make an easy-peasy fortune for not too much work. And—dreaming big again—the ongoing maintenance for five private boat docks would give him a steady stream of income doing seasonal repair work that he could depend on from here on out.

Quinn parked his bike on the cracked patio around the back of the sprawling bungalow-style house and killed the engine. Expecting silence, he was assaulted by a loud racket of braying, mooing, and barking.

"Are you kidding me?" He walked to the hedge separating his property from the annoying clamor. When he'd toured the property with Delia, it had been as peaceful as a church. She hadn't warned him it cozied up to Old McDonald's farm.

Or, maybe more accurately, Old Ms. McDonald's farm. He'd glimpsed the crazy-looking woman hiding in the shrubbery with her wild mane of honey-brown hair, ratty bathrobe, and cowboy boots. How the hell would he get top dollar for a house with an eccentric animal-hoarding neighbor next door? He stalked to the overgrown hedge between the properties and bellowed at the animals. "Shut. Up."

The noise level escalated exponentially. "Fork it," Quinn said, forgetting that without Sean here, he could've used the more satisfying expletive.

The multispecies chorus ramped it up. Parrots screeched loud enough to make the donkeys sound like amateurs. Parrots? "What next? Lions, tigers, and bears?"

Fine. He would work inside today. Quinn planned to get the pool house fit for habitation in time for Sean's scheduled visit next weekend—unless the kid canceled again, claiming homework, football practice, school projects, whatever.

All great excuses, but was that all they were? Excuses?

Did his son really hate him so much that he never wanted to see him again?

The thought hit Quinn in the solar plexus with the force of a fist. If it had been a woman treating him that way, he'd have gotten the message and moved on. But this was his *son*. His heart. The kid was fifteen now, so Quinn had only three years of court-mandated visitation to compel Sean to keep coming around.

Three years suddenly seemed like a very short time, given all the inattention and absence Quinn had to make up for. And yet, it had to be possible for him to retrace his steps and rebuild the bridge between him and his son.

Quinn was a carpenter, after all. He knew how to build anything, even a rickety, falling-apart bridge. And he would rebuild this one, no matter what it took. The fight for Sean's time and attention generated its own list of obstacles, but Quinn had ordered the first round of obstacle-climbing tools online:

1. Cool guy furniture.
2. Flat-screen TV.

3. Premium cable and internet.

4. Xbox game system.

5. Paddleboards (secondhand).

Quinn knew of only one way to close the distance between him and Sean that compounded daily—worse than credit-card debt—because of his ex-wife Melissa's subtle sabotage.

He must become the best weekend dad he could afford to be.

"Got you another one," Abby announced above the sound of the screen door slapping shut behind her. "Saw her run into the culvert when I took the trash up to the road."

Reva came into the kitchen, dressed in Birkenstocks and a tie-dyed hippie dress, her prematurely silver hair secured with an enormous jeweled barrette. "Oh my Lord." She set her suitcase by the sliding glass doors and reached for the kitten. "Just this one? No stragglers?"

"She's the only one I saw, but I'll keep a lookout in case there are others."

Reva held the kitten like a curled-up hedgehog between her palms. Her magic touch calmed the kitten, who immediately started purring. Reva closed her eyes, a slight frown line between her arched brows. "She's the only one." Reva opened her hazel-green eyes, her gaze soft-focused. "But kitten season has begun, and folks'll start dropping off puppies next. Are you sure you can handle this place by yourself all summer?"

No, not at all. Abby had only recently mastered the art of getting out of bed every morning. But Reva deserved this break, this chance to follow her dreams after years of helping everyone but herself. "Yes, of course I can handle it." She glanced at the kitchen clock. "Don't you need to leave soon?"

"No hurry. My friend Heather will pick me up after she drops her kids off at school, so rush hour will be over by the time we get into the city. And the New Orleans airport is small enough that I can get there thirty minutes before departure and still have plenty of time. It's all good."

Abby gave Reva a sideways look, but didn't say anything. Abby knew her aunt was excited about her upcoming adventure but equally afraid of reaching for a long-postponed dream she wasn't sure she'd be able to achieve. She might be stalling, just a little.

"What can I do to help you and your suitcase get out the door?"

"Would you get a big wire crate from storage and set it up for this baby?"

"Sure."

Cradling the purring kitten, Reva followed Abby through the laundry room to the storage closet. "Litter box is in the bottom cabinet, cubby for her to hide in is on the top shelf."

Abby hefted the folded wire crate. "Where should I put it?"

Reva closed her eyes again, doing her animal communication thing. "Not a big fan of dogs—or other cats either. Wants to be an only cat." Reva smiled and stroked the kitten's head. "You may have to adjust your expectations, little one, just like everyone else in the world."

Not exactly an answer, but Abby knew Reva would get around to it, and she did. "She'll need a quiet place away from the crowd for the first few days. Let's put the crate on top of the laundry room table."

While Abby set up the crate, Reva gave instructions. "Take her to the vet ASAP; she's wormy and needs antibiotics for this road rash. You can use one of the small travel crates for that. But other than the vet visit, keep her in here until next week, Wednesday at the earliest. Then you can move her crate to my worktable in the den. That'll get her used to all the activity around here. When she's had all her kitten shots, you can let her out into the general population."

Abby put a soothing hand on her aunt's arm. "I'll remember." She knew that Reva secretly thought no one else could manage the farm adequately—with good reason. This place was a writhing octopus of responsibilities. Critters to feed, stalls to clean, and two more weeks of school field trips to host before summer break. Even in summer, there would be random birthday parties and scout groups every now and then. No wonder Reva was having a hard time letting go; hence all the detailed instructions on how to handle the newest addition to the farm's family. "I promise I'll take good care of everything."

Reva gave a yes-but nod and a thanks-for-trying smile. "I'll text you a reminder about the kitten, just in case."

Of course you will. Reva had already printed a novel-length set of instructions on everything from animal-feeding to tour-hosting to house-and-barn maintenance. Smiling at Reva's obvious difficulty in releasing the need to control everything in her universe, Abby filled a water bowl from the mop sink and placed it inside the crate next to the food dish. "All set."

"Call me before you make that decision."

"What decision?" Reva had returned to a previous train of thought that had long since left the station in Abby's mind.

"About when to let the kitten out. She might be more squirrelly than she looks. Let me check in with her and make sure she's ready. Don't want to have her hiding under the couch or escaping into the woods through the dog door." Reva paused with a just-thought-of-something look on her face. "But I'd totally trust you to ask this kitten if she's ready to join the herd. This summer at the farm will be a good opportunity for you to practice your animal communication skills."

Right, well. Abby didn't trust herself, even though Reva had been tutoring her since Abby first started spending summers here as a child. "I'll call first. I'd like to keep the training wheels on a little longer if you don't mind."

Reva laughed. "Training wheels are not necessary. You just think you need them. You're a natural at animal communication."

Abby didn't feel like a natural at much of anything these days. The fact that Reva trusted her to run the farm all summer attested more to Reva's high motivation to get her license to care for injured wildlife than to Abby's competency. Three months of an internship at a wild animal refuge in south Florida would give Reva everything she needed to make that long-deferred dream a reality. Abby was determined to help out, even though the responsibility terrified her. It was the least she could do.

Reva tipped her chin toward the open shelves above the dryer. "Put one of those folded towels on the lid of the litter box so she can sit on top of it."

Abby obeyed, and Georgia started barking from outside. "That's probably your ride, Aunt Reva. I've got this, I promise. You don't have to worry." She held out her hands for the kitten.

Reva transferred the purring kitten gently into Abby's cupped palms. The kitten stopped purring, but settled quickly when Abby snuggled it close. "About time for you to go, right?"

Reva gave a distracted nod. "Don't forget to make the vet appointment today. You want to go ahead and get on their schedule for tomorrow, because they close at noon on Saturdays. But call before you go. I don't know why, but everyone at Mack's office has been really disorganized lately. The last time I went in, they had double-booked, and I had to wait over an hour."

"I will make the appointment today, and I'll call before I go."

"Oh, and don't forget to drop that check off at the water department when you're out tomorrow. Those effers don't give you a moment's grace before cutting off the water." A car horn blasted outside.

"I won't forget." Abby put the kitten in the crate and shooed her aunt out the door. "I'd hug you, but I'm all muddy."

"I know I'm forgetting something." Reva glanced around the room one last time. "Oh well. I'll text you if I remember." She leaned in and kissed Abby's cheek. "Bless you for doing this for me."

"I'm glad we can help each other. Don't worry about a thing." As if Reva wasn't the one doing Abby a big favor by giving her a place to stay when even her own parents refused, for Abby's own good. They were completely right when they pointed out that by the age of thirty-three, she should have gotten her shit together. After all, they'd had two good jobs, a solid (if unhappy) marriage, a kid, and a mortgage by that time of their lives.

It wouldn't have helped to argue that up until the moment she didn't, she'd also had a good job (dental office manager), an unhappy relationship (with the philandering dentist), and a kid (the dentist's five-year-old daughter). Okay, so she didn't have a mortgage. Points to Mom and Dad for being bigger adults at thirty-three. Whoopee. It was a different economy back then.

After Reva left, Abby showered and dressed to meet her first big challenge as the sole custodian of Bayside Barn—ushering in three school buses that pulled through the gates just after 9:00 a.m.

When the deep throb of the buses' motors vibrated the soles of her barn boots, Abby tamped down the familiar flood of anxiety that rose up her gut like heartburn. The feeling of impending disaster arose often, sometimes appearing out of nowhere for no particular reason. Only one of the reasons she'd come to stay at Aunt Reva's for a while. This time, though, she had reason to feel anxious. These three buses held a total of ninety boisterous kindergartners, enough to strike fear in the stoutest of hearts.

Abby hadn't forgotten Reva's warning about the timing of her tenure as acting director of Bayside Barn. Two weeks remained of the school year, and those last two weeks were always the worst; not only did schools schedule more trips then, but the kids would be more excitable and the teachers' tempers would be more frayed.

Abby hurried to get Freddy, the scarlet macaw, from his

aviary enclosure. "You can do this," she muttered to herself, remembering the Bayside Barn mission statement that Reva made all the volunteers memorize: *Bayside Barn will save the world, one happy ending at a time, by giving a home to abandoned animals whose unconditional love and understanding will teach people to value all creatures and the planet we share.*

If that wasn't a reason to get over herself and get on with it, nothing was.

Chapter 2

ABBY STROKED FREDDY'S FEATHERS ON THE WAY BACK TO the parking lot, soothing herself as much as him. She *could* do this. She had helped Aunt Reva host school field trips several times. And five seasoned helpers were here, women who knew the drill from years of experience. The choking sense of anxiety drifted down and hung like a fog, somewhere around the region of her kneecaps.

With the huge parrot perched on her shoulder, Abby joined her helpers—two retirees and three student-teachers from the local college. Each wore jeans and rubber-soled barn boots; each wore a different-colored T-shirt with the Bayside Barn Buddies logo on the front.

The ladies had already directed the bus drivers to park in the gravel lot between the light-blue farmhouse and the bright-red barn. Ninety boisterous kindergartners spilled out of the buses, and the donkeys brayed a friendly greeting over the barn fence. Freddy clung to Abby's shoulder with his talons and hollered in her ear, "Welcome, Buddies!"

The teachers and parent chaperones in the first bus corralled their kindergartners into small groups. The hellions that had spewed from the other two buses yelled and chased each other around the roped-off gravel parking area. Feeling more relaxed now that the field trip experience was underway, Abby gave the kids a minute to get their wiggles out, then removed a gym whistle from her jeans pocket and blew three short, sharp blasts. Everybody froze.

"Listen up." She tried to channel Aunt Reva's stern school-teacher voice. "Before we can begin, I need each of the teachers and parent chaperones to gather the kids in your group."

After a bit of shuffling, the crowd coalesced into small clusters of five-or-so kids surrounding each of the adults. A small swarm of kids milled around looking worried. Abby held up a hand. "Kids who aren't sure which group you belong to, please line up right here in front of me."

Within five minutes, every child had found the right group, and Abby's helpers handed out color-coded stickers, badges shaped like a sheriff's star surrounded by the words, *I'm a Bayside Barn Buddy.*

Abby blasted the whistle again. "Welcome to Bayside Barn. In a moment, you'll follow me to the pavilion where we'll watch a short video about the animals you will meet here today. Then, each group will go with the guide whose shirt matches your star. Together, you will learn and explore for the rest of the morning. We'll meet back at the pavilion at noon for lunch, and then you'll have another two hours of fun before you head back to school. Sound good?"

Abby allowed the chorus of excited talking to continue another minute. "Okay, everyone. Follow me to the pavilion."

She led the way with Freddy on her shoulder and Georgia walking alongside. A small hand crept into hers. A tiny, pigtailed girl with brown eyes as big as buckeyes skipped beside her. Abby swung the little girl's hand. "Hello there. What's your name?"

"Angelina. I like your bird. I ain't never seen a bird that big. Can I hold him on my shoulder like you're doin'?"

"I'm sorry, Angelina, but that wouldn't be safe. Freddy's a good bird, but if something startled him, he might bite."

"Where'd you get him?"

"All the animals at Bayside Barn came here because their families couldn't keep them."

Angelina stopped skipping and tugged Abby's hand. "My family couldn't keep me either. Can I come live here too?"

Abby's heart squeezed with the familiar breathlessness of regret. Regret for promises she'd made to a child she had loved completely and yet failed to save.

A frazzled-looking woman grabbed Angelina's arm, mumbled an apology, and towed the child back to her group.

Abby kept her eyes on the pavilion and kept walking. The fresh scratches the kitten had made on her hands and belly stung with every movement. But her small pains were worth it, since the kitten was safe and secure in the darkened laundry room with a clean litter box, a soft blanket, and plenty of food and water.

Abandoned kittens could be saved.

Abandoned children, not so easily.

—————

Quinn backed out from under the kitchen cupboard and shut off the shop vac. He sat back on his heels and listened. *What the hell...?*

He opened the sliding doors and looked across the pea-green pool water to the house next door. Over the tall hedges, he saw the tops of three school buses.

School buses, parked next door?

"Shit." That would account for the high-pitched screams and squeals. What kind of place had he moved next to?

Quinn clenched his jaw and pressed a thumb against his temple that throbbed as if someone had jabbed an ice pick into his head. His decision to sink every penny of his equity money into this place might have been a Very Bad Mistake.

After a lifetime of following his gut and making snap decisions that often had negative (okay, disastrous) consequences, Quinn had recently promised himself that from here on out, he'd write out the pros and cons of any major decision before making it. He'd done that before buying this estate.

Maybe the problem wasn't with his decision-making process. Maybe he was just good at finding gold and spinning it into straw.

He walked down the long gravel drive to the paved road and looked across the blacktop where a sea of yellow-flowering vines stretched to the distant horizon. It had seemed like such a grand idea to buy the crumbling estate across from all this wild extravagance. The invasive cat's-claw vine smothered trees and pulled down structures, creating a thriving and beautiful wasteland, the first of four selling points for the property he planned to flip:

1. Acres of yellow flowers across the street.

2. Bayside view at the back—with the potential for waterfront access.

3. Lonely country road on one side.

4. Only one neighboring property, well hidden
   behind an evergreen hedge.

He walked past that tall hedge to get a better look at the property next door. A double-panel iron gate stood open, flanking the entrance. A thick stone pillar surrounded an oversize mailbox. Under the mailbox, a brass plaque read:

Bayside Barn
8305 Winding Water Way

The ice pick jabbed into Quinn's skull again.

He remembered hearing about this place when Sean's class went here on a field trip in the third grade. Sean had come home sunburned, exhausted, and overexcited from a day at the barn and the hour-long bus ride to and from his elementary school in New Orleans. Sean had talked nonstop about the experience for the rest of the evening, then fallen asleep at the dinner table. For the rest of the month, he had galloped around the house every afternoon after school, waving a sou-venir cowboy hat and yelling, "Go, Bayside Buddies, go!"

The place next door was a damn zoo.

―――――――――

Reva stepped onto the horrifyingly long escalator to the ground transportation level, steadied herself as the step unfolded beneath her, then wrestled her too-big suitcase onto the step behind her as it, too, unfolded. She gripped the shud-dering plastic handrail and held on, closing her eyes for a blessed moment.

God, she missed her husband.

Grayson had always taken charge of, well, everything. When they traveled, he was the one who made the arrange-ments, knew where to go and when to be there, and wrangled their luggage along the way.

What the hell was she doing here, so far out of her com-fort zone that her heart hadn't stopped pounding since she left the house this morning? Did she even want to do this anymore? Without Grayson by her side, she felt untethered. Her parents were gone. Grayson's brother, Winston, and his wife—Abby's parents—had never warmed up to her. She and Grayson had made the decision not to have children, but to

devote their lives to something larger, a mission to help animals. They'd built Bayside Barn together on the homestead
he'd inherited from his grandparents.

This had been *their* dream. But was it still *hers*, if it
meant doing it all without him? Grayson had been a force of
nature, something between an exhilarating whirlwind and an
unavoidable undertow. When the neighbors next door had
moved into an assisted-living facility, Grayson convinced
the city council to buy the land for an animal shelter, which
she and Grayson would run. But then Grayson died, and the
penny-pinching mayor vetoed the plan. He didn't see the
upside of building an official animal shelter when the unoffi-
cial one at Bayside Barn worked well enough.

Without a doubt, Grayson's passion and vision would've
convinced the mayor to go along. With his whiskey-colored
eyes and lopsided grin, he could melt the hardest heart. God,
she had loved that man. Still did, always would. He'd been
gone almost two years, and Reva was still a little bit pissed
off at the universe for letting Grayson's unwavering commit-
ment to physical fitness lead to his own untimely death.

He had always teased her about her lack of interest in
physical exercise and healthy eating. He'd poke her soft belly
and claim that he would still love her when she got fat from

lounging in the pool with a glass of wine while he swam laps. She slept in and rested her other side while he put on his running shoes and logged his five miles each day.

And then came the knock on the door that woke her from a sound sleep the morning that an inattentive driver—

"Hey!" A big hand gripped her arm and steadied her when the escalator steps leveled out and she stumbled over the ledge that devoured each step. Her eyes flew open and she grabbed onto a man's hard shoulder as he dragged her and her suitcase away from the steps that were being swallowed by the floor. "Lady, are you okay?"

She looked into the concerned green eyes of a very tall, very young black man. He still held onto her, and she still held onto him. In fact, she was afraid that if she let go, she might crumple down to the floor. Her ankles felt boneless; her knees felt like Jell-O. "I'm so sorry. I swear I only closed my eyes for a second. I didn't know it would move so fast."

"No worries, lady." His strong, reassuring grip didn't lessen. "You look a little shaky. You okay?"

She held onto his arm and took stock of herself. Steadier, she let go and stepped back. "I'm okay. Thanks for keeping me from falling on my face—or my backside."

"Lucky thing I was standing down here watching you."

He smiled. "Not being a creep or anything; I'm waiting for my girlfriend to come down on her way to baggage claim. I noticed you because your face looked so...peaceful, I guess... like you were thinking of something beautiful."

She felt an answering smile bloom, first in her heart, and then on her lips. "You're right. I was."

The young man moved off to embrace his girlfriend, and Reva headed for the ground transportation exit. For the first time since she'd left the house this morning, she felt like she was doing the right thing, and that Grayson's spirit would support her in fulfilling the dream they had shared. It was only right that Abby should come to Bayside Barn for healing and, in turn, give Reva the space she needed to find a way to move forward in her own life.

In a way, Abby was the child Grayson and Reva never had. Ever since Abby had been old enough to spend the night away from home, she had spent her summers at Bayside Barn. That old homestead was in her bones, and the animals that lived there were her childhood friends. Reva knew that Abby would take care of the farm and the animals as well as Reva could. And maybe the experience would deepen Abby's connection to the animals and allow her to practice her ability to communicate with them telepathically. Reva had shown her how, and though Abby's parents did their best to undo that teaching, Reva knew that Abby possessed the ability.

Abby hadn't embraced her gifts yet, but one day, she would. One day, Abby would receive a communication that couldn't be denied or passed off as her imagination. Reva wished she could do more to help Abby recognize her abilities. But as Grayson had told her many times, "You can't push the river." She could only toss seeds upon the water and hope they would float to a fertile place that would support their growth.

Still feeling Grayson's presence beside her, Reva wheeled her suitcase out a set of double doors to a curbside pickup lane that smelled of car exhaust and stale cigarette smoke.

At the preappointed spot, a spindly, bored-looking man wearing camo pants and a plain green shirt leaned against a white-paneled van. Reva had expected a vehicle with a logo for the wildlife center on the side, but this looked more like a prison van. All her insecurities and doubts about the wisdom of leaving home for so long rose up to choke her, but she swallowed them down. "Hello?"

Immersed in his cell phone and his cigarette, the van guy seemed not to notice her. He took a slow drag from his cigarette, blew the smoke out sideways, then looked at her through one squinting eye. "Sorry. I'm a little hard of hearing. Come again?"

She spoke a little louder. "Is this the transport van to the wildlife refuge?"

"Yep, and you're the last to load up." He dropped his cigarette and ground it into the pavement with his boot. "You ready?"

She remembered the feeling of being protected and guided by Grayson, and she pulled that feeling around her like a blanket until she almost felt as if his hand rested at her waist. "I'm ready."

The driver hauled her suitcase into the back of the van, then waited while she dug into her purse and brought out a few dollars to plunk into his palm. He pocketed the money and grinned. "Get on in."

The row seats behind the driver were all filled with college-age students, many of whom had backpacks taking up the space beside them. Reva hovered in the van's open doorway. "Hello, everyone. I'm Reva. It's nice to meet y'all."

A chorus of unenthusiastic "hey" and "hi" and "hello" responses were even further diminished by the fact that only one of Reva's fellow passengers managed to look up from their cell phones. But from the middle seat, a pretty girl with purple-tipped dreadlocks waved and smiled. "Hey. I'm Dana. You can sit next to me."

Dana scooted closer to the window and stowed her backpack under the seat. Reva squeezed past the beefy guy with military-short blond hair on the end of the row to take the middle seat.

Startled, he looked up from his phone, then smiled. "Oh, hey." He took out one earbud and moved his long legs out of her way. "Come on through."

Reva got settled, then held out a hand and introduced herself to each of the kids in her row. As the van trundled out of the Miami International Airport complex, the kids in the two other rows looked up from their devices and started chatting with one another. A girl from the back put a hand on Reva's shoulder and introduced herself. A guy from the front turned around and said hi. Feeling more included, Reva relaxed. She reminded herself that kids these days used their phones as a way of coping with social anxiety the way she had once kept her nose buried in a book.

Once the van passed the brightly lit streets and began to bump along dark highways and back roads toward their final destination, everyone disappeared again into their electronic devices. She turned to her own cell phone for solace as well.

Hey, Abby, she typed. My flight landed safely and I'm on my way to the internship. Wish me luck! I hope everything's going well back at the farm. How was the school tour today? How is the new kitten? Did you get an appointment at the vet's office for tomorrow?

She hit Send, then tucked her cell phone into her purse's side pocket. Then she stared out the window at endless pine forests until the lumbering lurch of the van lulled her to sleep.

―――――――――――

Quinn put on his headphones, turned up the volume on his playlist, and began the painstaking process of regrouting the vintage floor tiles in the pool-house bathroom.

First, he scraped out the top layer of the old grout with a grout saw—a small, handheld, inefficient tool that made his hands cramp.

The whole time he did it, he fumed.

How in the hell was he going to sell this place for a profit with a damn petting zoo next door? He might've just sunk a bunch of money—the last of his money, in fact—into a horrible mistake. Even after agonizing over all the potential pros and cons, he had failed to uncover a bigger con than all of his worst imaginings.

He scraped grout until his knees ached from inching along on the hard floor. Then he applied new grout, using a float to smash the gritty goop into the lines and smooth it level.

Why would Delia sell him this place without full disclosure of a deal-breaking drawback? Had she deliberately shown the property on a weekend knowing that weekdays sounded like schoolyard-playground mayhem all day long?

He pulled out one earbud to check if the mayhem was still ongoing.

Yes. The screaming went on all fucking day long.

"Time for a break." He would have to let the grout set for exactly thirty minutes before wiping off the hazy residue. His knees creaked when he stood with all the grace of an elderly monk rising from another round of useless prayers. When he reached out to steady himself on the doorframe, his fingers felt like sandpaper on the smooth painted surface. The grout had sucked all the moisture out of his skin. His hands felt— and looked—like the Sahara in dry season.

He had earned a beer by the nasty green pool. Yes indeed, his crepe-dry fingers assured him, he had.

But the beer he opened by the pool lacked the promise of respite, because any hope of relaxation was swamped by the happy shrieks of children running and playing next door.

And, good God, was one of the little heathens climbing the hedge-covered chain-link fence between the two properties?

Quinn stood and stalked to the hedge, which some grimy-faced young boy had just managed to conquer. The kid's triumphant gap-toothed grin faltered a fraction when his eyes locked with Quinn's hostile gaze. "Hello, misther," the kid lisped as his spindly body draped over the hedge's bowing branches. "Don't be mad. I'm just playin' around."

"How 'bout you just play around on the other side of the fence where you're supposed to be? I'd hate to have to tattle to your teacher."

The kid looked over his shoulder and back again. "You don't know my teacher."

"Wanna bet?" Quinn pulled his cell phone from his back pocket and started punching in random numbers. "I know her well enough to know that she'll make you sit by yourself in the bus for the rest of the day while everyone else gets to have fun at the farm."

The boy's eyes opened wide. "Please, misther. Don't tell her. Don't…" He backpedaled and fell off the hedge with an "Oomph."

Quinn stepped onto a sturdy low-hanging branch and looked over the hedge to make sure the kid hadn't been hurt when he fell. Apparently not; all churning elbows and trailing shoelaces, he was sprinting back to the safety of the group.

Quinn hopped off the hedge, then chuckled and took a sip of his beer.

But his mirth was short-lived. If the current commotion next door was any indication, no matter how much money, time, and effort he sank into this place, the perfect buyer he had imagined would never materialize. He had thought that it would be a recently retired couple. His mind's eye had conjured the visual of a stout man who enjoyed fishing and a plump woman who enjoyed gardening.

The man would launch his aluminum fishing boat from the adjacent dead-end street that ended in a cracked concrete boat ramp—or from their own private boat dock if Quinn managed to acquire the waterfront land. The woman would sit by the pool and read romance novels. She'd use a monogrammed shovel from Restoration Hardware to plant daylilies in the estate's rich, well-drained soil, an ideal mix of sand and silt washed up from the bay for the last hundred years.

Quinn was pretty sure that neither of those imagined retirees would be enthused about the idea of baby hoodlums climbing the hedge, falling into the pool, and drowning so the kids' parents could sue them for everything they'd worked for all their lives.

He sat in the folding stadium chair and kept an eye on the empty hedge. Feeling antsy and unfulfilled, haunted by the image of the perfect retired couple and the futility of renovating a property they'd never decide to purchase, he made a quick decision. No time for making a list of pros and cons; something had to be done. It had to be done now, and it might require drastic measures.

Chapter 3

QUINN HAD INVESTED EVERYTHING IN THIS PLAN TO MOVE here and rebuild his reputation, his life, and his relationship with his son. He could have turned his back on the past, bought a condo in the Keys, and left all his regrets behind. But one thing—one person, his son, to be exact—held him back. If there was any small sliver of a chance that he could be a part of Sean's life, he had to take it.

He dialed the realty office, and some peon answered on the second ring, her voice way too chirpy for his taste. *Blah, blah, blah*—he held the phone away from his ear until she got to the important part: "How may I help you?"

He might have unloaded some of his frustration on the poor receptionist, but whatever. Anyway, within minutes he was speaking with the agent who'd sold him this piece-of-shit property.

"Delia," he roared. "Were you aware…" He went off on her about how he'd gambled everything on his plan to flip this property and make a sorely needed profit. She knew all this already, but it felt good to vent.

To her credit, she listened and said nothing but "Um-hmm, I hear you" until he'd worn himself out talking.

He needed a win. Goddammit, he'd been doing nothing but losing for so long, he needed—no, he deserved—a win. "Look," he finished. "I won't be able to flip this estate—and you won't be able to make the commission you'd been hoping for on the resale—unless we get rid of the petting zoo next door. What do you propose to do about this problem?"

She talked for a while about zoning and variances and grandfathered permissions to keep livestock on land that had been annexed into the city of Magnolia Bay.

"I don't care about any of that." He took another healthy swig of beer. "I just want you to fix the problem. Call City Hall. Circulate a petition. Do whatever you have to do. Just get that damn zoo gone. I have to be able to sell this place to a nice retired couple who can afford to buy it."

"Quinn, I've known you for almost a year." Had sex with him a few times too. "And I know you don't really mean what you're saying right now. Can't you just talk to your neighbor and work it out?"

"You want me to go over there and say, 'Pretty please, stop making your living the way you have been for the last decade or so?' How well do you think that'll go over?"

Delia whined about the time and effort and red tape involved in rescinding grandfathered permissions to keep farm animals in the city limits.

"I don't care," he said again. "You showed me this place on a quiet Sunday afternoon, and I'll bet you scheduled the showing then for a reason."

"Aw, Quinn, come on. Stop being dramatic."

"Come on yourself, Delia. You never even answer your phone on the weekends. I should have known something was up when you couldn't meet me here during the week."

She declined to respond to that one. "I guess you need to vent, Quinn, so go ahead. I'll listen till you're done."

"Your lack of candor has caused me a big problem, and you need to fix it." If he couldn't sell this place, the money he had squirreled away for renovations wouldn't be worth a thin dime. "Tell you what. I'll pay you a ten-thousand-dollar bonus when you sell this estate for double what I paid for it. That's on top of your normal commission." He paused for a minute to let that sink in. "And remember that other little property you told me about." Quinn gazed out over the landscape where a hundred acres of marshland met the bay. "If and when it goes up for sale, we can both quadruple our profits. Now. Can you, or can you not, make the zoo next door go away?"

He heard her take a breath, then let it out.

"Well?" He took another pull at his beer, only to find that the bottle was empty.

"I'll do what I can," she said. "If I can."

"Fine. I'll trust you to handle it, for your benefit as well as mine."

"I will," Delia answered. "I'll handle it."

"Good. Keep me posted." Now that he had vented, he felt much more relaxed and easygoing than he had a half hour before. He strolled into the pool house, dumped the empty bottle in the kitchen's recycle bin, then went to wipe down the bathroom tiles.

He hummed and scrubbed, clinging to his pie-in-the-sky vision of the retired couple who would enjoy their happily-ever-after lives in the dream home he was determined to create here.

That evening, Abby dumped the day's trash bags into the can
by the road, thinking about the *For Sale* sign the motorcycle
dude had discarded in the weeds in front of the neighboring estate. She had completely forgotten to tell Aunt Reva,
and maybe that was a good thing, because Reva deserved at
least a few days of bliss before hearing that the animal shelter she'd been campaigning for would never happen. Abby
slammed the trash-can lid. "Oh well."

Reva had begged the Magnolia Bay City Council to buy
the abandoned estate next door and convert it into a much-
needed animal shelter for the city. She had even offered to run
the shelter as an extension of Bayside Barn, since all the strays
got dumped there, anyway.

Abby looked down at Georgia. "Any bright ideas from the
canine quarter?"

Georgia, as usual, was on it. She tunneled through the tall
grass toward the downed sign. Her gray speckles and black
spots disappeared in the vegetation, but her white-tipped tail
waved above the tasseled grasses, setting dandelion seeds free
in the warm Louisiana air. After a minute or two of consideration, she came back grinning as if a direct line to the powers
that be had assured her everything would be okay.

Abby wasn't so sanguine, but Reva's dog encouraged

her to take the long view. "You think the city will buy the marshland behind here instead?" Not likely, since the bayside marshland behind the estates on this road wasn't for sale. In addition, the water-soaked bog filled with snakes and alligators was unsuitable for anything but a great view unless someone had a fortune to spend on fill dirt.

In other words, the land was unavailable, unsuitable, unattainable. Sort of like the men in Abby's life.

Bored with the ongoing conundrum, Georgia crossed the blacktop and sniffed at a tangle of smothering vines that edged the easement. While beautiful, cat's-claw could strangle every living thing for miles, and it had made a good start here.

Georgia growled and peered into the vine-covered forest with her hackles up.

"What's with the mean fur?" Abby imagined a pair of predatory gold eyes staring through the vines, watching. A chill poured through her. The fine hairs on her arms rose and she shivered. *Cat walking over your grave*, Reva would've said.

Abby scolded herself the way her mom always had. "Abby Curtis, your imagination is as wild as your hair. There are no cougars or wolves in Louisiana."

The eerie feeling of being watched wasn't just Abby's imagination, though. Georgia felt it too. The little dog barked at whatever was hiding in the cat's-claw, threatening it with a don't-make-me-come-in-there-and-get-you tone.

"Come on, girl," Abby coaxed. "Let's go home."

Without warning, Georgia darted into the forest, sounding an alarm that would make most animals exit the scene immediately. But Georgia's barking came from a fixed location now. God only knew what poor creature cowered on the receiving end of her scolding. Not more kittens; Georgia never barked at cats. Probably a snake...

Abby's ever-present stream of worry escalated into a roaring river of panic. "Georgia!"

———————

Wolf sat on his haunches under the canopy of vines. The little multicolored dog shot into the cat's-claw forest and charged at him. Hackles raised, she lowered her copper eyebrow spots into a fierce scowl and growled. "You don't belong here."

Wolf looked away, showing deference.

Georgia advanced. "What are you doing here? Go away."

Wolf hunkered down and crawled backward, retreating farther into the shadows. He refused to meet the challenge in her intelligent brown eyes, but he tried to use his body language to send a message of peace. "I won't hurt you."

"You aren't supposed to be here," she insisted. "Go home."

He eased back until his tail brushed the front wall of the half-roofed house hidden beneath the grasping vines. He'd been sheltering here ever since his human caretaker drove him far from home and shoved him off the back of the truck.

Discarded in disgrace.

He didn't understand why, even after days of hunger and thirst and thinking, thinking, thinking.

The woman's voice called out. "Georgia. Get back here, now." Beneath the command was fear, concern, love. His chest felt as heavy as the water-filled doormat he had once—in his exuberant puppyhood—dragged off the porch and torn up.

The dog named Georgia looked back but didn't retreat. "You don't belong here. Go home."

Wolf lowered his elbows to the ground and flattened himself in submission. He sent a silent message to Georgia. "I can't go home. I am being punished. My people left me here, and I think they will come back for me. I have to wait."

Georgia sat, panting. "What did you do wrong?"

Wolf didn't know. He waited for Georgia to ask a different question he might know the answer to.

"Georgia," the woman's voice called out, still high-pitched

with anxiety but softer and sweeter than before. "Girlfriend, what are you doing in there?"

Her voiceless reply: "I am talking to the gold-eyed dog-thing."

So. She could tell he wasn't fully dog or fully wolf. She turned her fierce gaze on him, but the white tip of her thick brown tail flickered a greeting.

"Georgia." The woman's voice sounded sharp again, the tone veering between fear and love. "Get back here."

Georgia stood. "Abby is calling me. I do what I want, but it is time for me to go. You can stay." She turned tail and trotted back to the woman.

Wolf put his head on his paws and ignored the hungry rumbling of his belly.

———

With a last parting shot in the one-sided argument, Georgia bounded out of the cat's-claw, her gray speckled coat covered in damp yellow petals.

Abby's concern evaporated. "Did you tell 'em?"

Georgia sneezed, a gesture that looked like an emphatic *yes*.

"Good. Can we please go home now?" Abby waited for

Georgia to trot past, then closed the wrought-iron gate and fastened the padlock. "What in the world were you barking at?"

Georgia danced around Abby's feet, whining and yipping as if she had important information to share.

Reva claimed that anyone could communicate with animals, and she'd given Abby a hundred thousand short tutorials. But as Reva had often said, practice and trust were essential ingredients, and Abby had to admit that she hadn't provided either of them. So if Georgia was trying to say something, Abby didn't get it. She petted the good dog's silky head. "Whatever it was, I'm sure you took care of it."

But an image of watchful gold eyes made Abby's shoulders twitch. Georgia barked, tail wagging, reminding Abby that daylight was fading fast. "You're right. It's time to feed critters and toss the ball."

In the big barn with its hand-painted sign—*Welcome, Bayside Barn Buddies*—above the open double doors, Abby poured feed into various bowls and buckets, humming along with the faint melody coming from the new neighbor's stereo. It played loud enough for her to hear the tune, but not loud enough for her to recognize the words. After seeing him on that motorcycle, dressed in black leather, she might have expected him to be the sort to play abrasive music with abusive lyrics loud enough to rattle the windows.

Maybe he would be a good neighbor to Aunt Reva, who had never quite fit in here in Magnolia Bay. Though she had married a born-and-bred resident of the area, her hippie clothing and unusual talent of telepathic animal communication made most people around here act a little standoffish. When Reva's husband died two years ago, her chance of blending into the clannish community died too. A good neighbor next door would be a blessing for Reva, and Abby should do whatever she could to facilitate that relationship.

She should bake a loaf of the secret-family-recipe pound cake and offer it to the new guy as a welcome to the neighborhood. It's what Reva would have done. Even though she wasn't really accepted around here, Reva remained unfailingly polite to everyone.

Removing her barn boots, Abby set them in the boot tray inside the back door, then padded into the old-fashioned farm kitchen and poured a glass of merlot.

Georgia sat, front paws in prayer position, a blue tennis ball in her mouth.

"You're right. It's ball time. But let's check on the kitten first." Abby went into the white-tiled laundry room with

Georgia at her heels. The kitten growled and spat and hissed, all the purring and promise of yesterday forgotten.

"Baby," Abby chided. When she stuck her fingers through the bars, hoping to calm the kitten with a caress, it scrambled into the cardboard hideout, knocking over the food dish on the way. Georgia set the ball down long enough to eat the scattered kibble off the floor. Then she snatched up the ball and streaked through the dog door onto the pool patio.

"Right behind you," Abby promised. She set her wine-glass on the dryer and stripped naked, then threw her clothes in the washer and turned it on. She took her swimsuit off the hook by the door—and had an epiphany. She was alone here! She could go naked if she wanted to. She hung the swimsuit back up and grabbed a towel. Feeling a slightly naughty sense of exhilaration at her secret indecency, she carried her wine outside and eased into the gently bubbling hot tub. Naked. Totally and completely naked.

It seemed like she was the only human in the universe.

So why couldn't she manage to relax? She ducked under-water to get her hair wet, then slid up onto the seat, tipped her head back, and willed her tense body to let go. Every muscle, every tendon, every molecule was clenched like a fist ready for battle.

Georgia dropped the ball and nosed it toward Abby's wineglass. Abby tossed the ball a few dozen times, then plunked it into the hot tub where Georgia wouldn't go. "No more playing."

Georgia settled on her haunches, elbows to the ground and feet pointing straight ahead in the classic cattle-dog pose. Eyeing the floating ball the way her ancestors had once eyed flocks of sheep, she waited patiently for Abby to make the next move.

Abby sipped her wine and surveyed her aunt's domain. Three—no, four—cats lounged within sight: Max, the big, gray tabby; Princess Grace, the elegant Siamese mix; Glenn, the black-and-white-spotted feral with a notched ear; and Jessie, another gray tabby with a notched ear. The others were all off doing cat things. Across the fence that separated the parking lot from the blue clapboard farmhouse, the petting-zoo animals rested in the big, red barn. Down the hill toward the bay, an owl hooted, answered by its mate a short distance away.

If Reva had been here, she would have told Abby what the owls were saying. "I'm here," probably. And "I'm here too." Animals weren't always running off at the mouth like humans. Most often, their calls back and forth were quick check-ins establishing location and well-being.

Family keeping up with family.

Something her parents had never seemed interested in. When Abby spent summers with Reva and Grayson, her parents hardly ever called. When Abby graduated from high school, they exchanged their three-bedroom house for a top-of-the-line home on wheels and offered to pay a year of storage fees for her stuff until she could "get the hang of adulting." When she graduated from college with a business degree, they didn't come; they'd been too busy avoiding the hot Louisiana summer by touring every campsite in Oregon.

When Abby cut herself adrift from her own life, she should've known to ask Reva for help first. Reva was a generous and forgiving Mother Earth, while Abby's father (Reva's brother-in-law) made Narcissus look like a philanthropist. Abby's mother, well, she was more like a ghost. Even when she was there, she wasn't really. Winston Curtis was the dense magnetic planet that kept his wife's dimming star from spinning off into oblivion. Whatever he said, she echoed, because she wasn't a whole person without him. Full of their customary thimbleful of compassion, they had advised Abby to tighten her bootstraps.

So when she found herself sitting in a leaking dinghy

watching her bridges burn behind her, and her parents had given unhelpful advice but no actual help, Abby had asked her aunt Reva for a patch of uncharred earth on which to land. "Yes, of course," her aunt had replied without skipping a heartbeat. "You're welcome to stay for as long as you like."

Family taking care of family.

Abby thought of the little girl she'd met today—Angelina—and hoped that if the child couldn't be with her family, at least she lived with people who loved her. Everyone, human or animal, deserved a home in which they knew unconditional love and acceptance. Abby thought of the child she'd had to leave behind in order to save herself, and swallowed a mouthful of wine along with the worry and regret that never left her mind. That it wasn't *her* child didn't make it better.

With the comforting bulk of the house behind her, Abby leaned her head back and let her feet float up. A couple of early stars winked on in the deepening sky, and solar lights glittered off to the left, lighting a flagstone path to the aviary and the pavilion. Straight ahead and down the hill, a fenced pasture surrounded the swimming hole whose brown water glittered dimly as the sun's last ray disappeared beyond the horizon.

The granddaddy oak Abby remembered from every summer of her childhood stood guard over the wooden dock. Fifty feet up into its fern-covered branches, a tire swing's hefty rope was tied so older kids could swing far out over the pond before letting go.

Beyond, rolling pastureland led down to a wide strip of marshland that bordered the bay a few miles away. A boat's motor made a whining sound in the distance; someone night fishing or checking trotlines.

Abby heard a munching sound and peered into the gathering shadows. At the property line between her aunt's farm and the new neighbor's estate, two long, curving horns bobbed in rhythm—a goat with his head buried in the privacy hedge. "Gregory." Out again, that bad, adventurous goat. "You could teach Houdini a thing or two."

Ignoring the goat—she could figure out how he'd gotten out of the pasture and into the yard tomorrow—Abby stood and set her empty wineglass next to her towel. The cooling night air tingled on her bare skin, raising goose bumps. She stepped onto the diving board, bounced a few times, and dove into the cool water.

Quinn sat by the pool in the gathering dusk. The frogs' mating song blended nicely with his new favorite song, "Any Man in America."

He felt kind of bad that tomorrow he would destroy the frogs' happy habitat with pool chemicals and a scrub broom. But maybe frogs also needed to learn about getting too comfortable and feeling too safe.

The Blue October song ended. Silence...then a strange rustling noise in the privacy hedge. Was crazy Old Ms. McDonald snooping on him? He eased to his feet and padded over, planning to surprise the old bat.

The hedge shook. He pulled apart a couple branches and met two blue eyes with strange-shaped pupils. He jumped back. *What the fork?*

He bent down and encountered a devil's face, complete with horns. "*Maaa*," the thing bellowed.

"I'll be damned." Quinn picked up a stick and poked it through the hedge-covered chain-link fence, right into the goat's nose.

"*Maaa...*" The goat bolted, leaving a perfect, goat-head-sized peephole into his new neighbor's backyard.

The sparkling-clean pool glowing blue, lit from within.

The kidney-shaped patio surrounded by globe lights.

His next-door neighbor's perfectly proportioned body diving naked into the swimming pool.

"Whoa." Quinn stumbled back, tripped over something, and fell on his ass.

He wouldn't be able to think of her as Old Ms. McDonald anymore.

Chapter 4

IT DIDN'T SURPRISE QUINN THAT HE HAD TROUBLE FALLING asleep that night, even though he had worked hard all day. Visions of his neighbor's slim, toned body and wavy brown hair followed him into fitful dreams.

In the first dream, she popped up from his frog-filled pool and wrapped her green-scaled mermaid arms around his neck. Pulling him into the murky depths, she showed him her magical cave of hidden delights. He knew she intended to keep him there forever, and he wanted to stay, until he realized with a shock that he couldn't breathe underwater.

Lungs convulsing, he broke free and kicked for the surface, but strong tendrils of seaweed dragged him down. He hacked at the seaweed, which turned into the dismembered arms and grasping fingers of all the other men she had lured under and destroyed.

He woke gasping for air, his legs tangled in the stiff, dye-smelling sheets on his new king-size bed. He got up and staggered to the kitchen, where he drank some water and shook off the lingering shreds of the dream's strange eroticism. When he went back to bed, sleep eluded him at first. He flipped and flopped like a gutted fish until the deep-throated burp of mating bullfrogs sang him back to sleep.

In the next dream, the woman next door wore the same yellow bathrobe and cowboy boots he'd seen her in this morning. She stood beside his bed, her hawklike eyes devouring him, but he didn't care. He knew she had some kind of mojo that was working on him, but he lacked the power to resist whatever magic she possessed.

Willing to die, he flung back the sheets.

She dropped the yellow robe and straddled him, her muddy boots digging into the new mattress. She rode him hard, waving a cowboy hat and yelling "Go, Bayside Buddy, go!"

Exhausted, he woke after dawn, disturbed by the strident wails of restless donkeys. He kicked free of the twisted sheets and sat on the edge of the bed.

Maybe he should admit defeat, sell this place for exactly

what he'd paid, and go to work for another builder. Who cared about all the time and money spent getting his contractor's license? Who cared about crafting his own business as an independent contractor? Who cared about polishing up this old gem of an estate and reselling at a hefty profit?

Unfortunately, he cared.

Flipping this place and making a profit wasn't just about flipping this place and making a profit. It was about rebuilding his relationship with his son. It was about showing his ex-wife that she'd made an even bigger mistake than he had. It was about making a new life for himself in Magnolia Bay and establishing his construction company as a valued member of the business community.

He couldn't quit now. He couldn't quit ever. He had to make this thing work.

While the coffee perked, he ate a slice of cold, leftover pizza and slipped a granola bar into his back pocket for later. With a decent playlist drowning out the zoo sounds, he carried a strong cup of black coffee and a legal pad outside. He sat in a folding stadium chair by the murky green pool and made his to-do list.

1. Get the truck and empty out the crappy apartment.

2. Drop off the apartment key.

3. Unload the truck.

4. Buy pool chemicals, weed killer, telescoping
   loppers.

5. Buy mortar and sand to fill cracks in the
   brick facing.

With a plan in place and caffeine in his system, Quinn felt slightly less like killing himself. He battled through a tangle of trees and vines and weeds to the property's edge. The distant view of the bay reassured him that he hadn't made a horrible mistake. Despite the noisy neighbor, this place sparkled with possibility and had the potential to triple or even quadruple his investment.

As long as he could find a buyer who suffered from significant hearing loss.

━━━━━━━━━

Abby woke to the donkeys' loud, discontented braying. Disoriented, she sat up and glanced at the clock. "Shit." She rocketed out of bed like a pebble from a slingshot, dumping Georgia and Max the tabby onto the floor.

Nine a.m. already. The donkeys complained for good

reason. Saturday morning coffee by the pool would have to wait. Her phone, plugged in by the bedside, displayed a slew of text messages, not that she had time to view or respond to them right now.

And wasn't there something else she was supposed to do today? She looked around the bedroom and chewed on a fingernail, waiting for her brain to kick in—and it did, sending a flood of adrenaline to her belly. *Shit!* She'd forgotten to call the vet's office yesterday. "Calm down," she said out loud. "It's not the end of the world."

The vet closed at noon on Saturdays, and that was their busiest day of the week. It would be too late to get an appointment now. Maybe that was just as well; it would take till noon to get the morning chores done. She promised herself that she'd make the call first thing Monday morning.

In the Daffy Duck boxer shorts and faded tank top she'd slept in, she put on barn boots and headed outside with Georgia and Max. When she walked into the barn, the hollering donkeys and ponies hollered even louder. A swarm of cats leaped onto the wide shelf above the food bins, yowling in anticipation.

Moving quickly, Abby scooped food from painted metal bins into matching color-coded buckets. (Aunt Reva had left nothing to chance.) Abby filled a green five-gallon bucket for the goats and sheep, a red one for the geese, chickens, ducks, and peacocks. Then, the single buckets: blue for each of the ponies. A pink one for the bunnies' communal bowl. Purple for the mini zebu, and orange for the potbellied pig.

She fed the whining donkeys first. Outside in the chicken yard, she scattered chicken scratch and left the gate open so the chickens and ducks and peacocks could spend the day foraging. She fed the aviary birds and hosed down their concrete floors, then tossed flakes of hay into the pastures and let the barn animals out to graze.

Sweaty and tired, Abby decided shoveling poop could wait until after coffee. She set up the coffeepot and hit the button to perk. She had just removed her boots when a deep bellow of human rage galvanized Georgia, who sprinted across the yard and squeezed under the fence. A second later, her sharp barking joined the new neighbor's angry expletives. Abby ran barefoot along the hedgerow fence toward Georgia's hysterical barking.

A donkey's cry made her heart race. How had Elijah gotten into the neighbor's yard? Then she saw how. "Oh shit." She climbed over a section of crumpled wire fencing and burst through a thick tangle of vegetation into a scene of mayhem and hysteria.

The new neighbor charged toward Elijah and flung his hands in the donkey's face. "Shoo. Get out."

Elijah reared, eyes rolling, ears pinned back. Abby grabbed a stout stick and rushed to defend her aunt's traumatized donkey. "Stop! You're scaring him."

Bawling in terror, Elijah veered around the man's waving arms and leaped over the crumpled wire fence. Georgia—all thirty pounds of short, snarling protection—stood between Abby and the crazy neighbor.

This man would not be getting any of the secret-family-recipe pound cake.

Holding the stick out like a sword, Abby snatched Georgia up one-handed and held her close. While she and the dog both trembled with reaction, Abby glared at her aunt's new neighbor. "What is wrong with you? You scared that poor donkey half to death."

The stupid Neanderthal crossed his muscled arms in front of his wide chest. "Me? You're asking what's wrong with me? That big moose knocked me down!"

"Moose? Elijah is just a baby! He would never—"

"He stole my granola bar!"

"He stole...what?"

The man glanced at her stick. Like a warrior calculating

his advantage in an armed conflict, he advanced, his expression fierce and his blue eyes so wild she could see the whites all around. "Your baby—who is the size of a moose, by the way—came onto my property, knocked me down, bit me on the ass, and stole a granola bar from my back pocket."

Georgia trembled in Abby's arms and growled in promised retribution should the man come close enough for her to reach.

Abby clutched the dog tighter. "I'm sorry if he hurt you. But you didn't have to scare him."

"Your ass is fine. Mine's the one that's been wounded." He lunged forward and wrenched the stick from her hand, then tossed it aside, ignoring Georgia's escalating growl. "And yet you're planning to attack *me* with a stick?"

A hysterical giggle tickled the back of Abby's throat. She bit her lips and patted Georgia. Laughing in the face of an animal-hating psychopath—maybe not the best move. "Yes, you're right. I'm sorry. I hope your..." She smothered an irreverent snort. "I hope your ass will recover."

His lips twitched, a quickly stifled smile. "I guess it will, eventually." He let the smile have its way, and it transformed his face from surly to sexy. Straight white teeth and deep blue eyes contrasted with deeply tanned skin. His sun-bleached brown hair hadn't been combed this morning; he looked like a man who'd just tumbled out of bed and wouldn't mind getting right back in, given sufficient motivation.

Not that she was interested in providing any such motivation. Hadn't she learned her lesson? Hadn't losing everything—her job, her self-respect, and the child she'd come to love—hadn't that experience taught her anything?

It most certainly had. She was done with men. Done.

He crossed unfairly muscular arms over unfairly toned abs. "Enjoying the view?"

Her face heated. "Well enough." She couldn't deny that she'd been staring. But her appreciation of his well-developed form was purely academic.

"Only fair, I guess." He swept an appreciative glance from her bare feet to her heated cheeks. His blue eyes shining with humor, he trapped her gaze in his. "I bought this place for the view, but I didn't know until recently what a bargain I was getting."

"Oh?" She glanced down at her dirt-smeared attire, a getup not likely to inspire such a flattering comment. Had he seen her yesterday with her robe gaping open? Or worse... Had he seen her skinny-dipping last night?

Nah. It would be impossible to see through that thick

hedge. As usual, Abby was letting her anxiety take over her mind and churn out scenarios of disaster. *Disasterizing*, Reva called Abby's newfound tendency to imagine the worst possible outcome and then dwell on it.

Georgia wiggled to get down, and Abby obliged. The dog toddled over and sniffed the guy's boots, then the hem of his jeans. Tail wagging, she returned to Abby and sat.

"Oh." Georgia had introduced herself; Abby should do the same. Without Georgia in her arms, Abby became uncomfortably aware of her unbound breasts thinly covered by the sloppy tank top, but etiquette demanded that she step forward and offer her hand. "I'm Abby. This is my aunt's place, but I'm in charge for the summer while she attends a summer internship to—"

Abby cut herself off. She was babbling, giving too much information that he didn't care to hear. Another symptom of the overwhelming anxiety that had plagued her after one poor decision derailed her entire life.

She tried again to act more like a normal person and less like a semi-hysterical nincompoop. "Welcome to the neighborhood."

He took her hand and smiled into her eyes. "I'm Quinn. Thanks for the welcome, unconventional as it was."

His touch ignited something inside her: a tiny flame she thought had been extinguished. A flame that needed to stay extinguished until she gained some control over her life. She withdrew her hand. "I'd better get back."

She hobbled barefoot over the stick-covered ground toward the crumpled fence. Without the flood of adrenaline that had propelled her here, the skinned-up soles of her bare feet flinched at every step.

His hand at her elbow offered support. "Are you okay?"

She smiled up at him. "Yep, yep, yep. I always run around barefoot in briars. You should see the soles of my feet. Tough as shoe leather." Her mind cringed at her runaway mouth. *Shut up. Shut. Up.*

He escorted her to the fence and helped her step over. Georgia slipped through a gap underneath.

"I'm very sorry that Elijah trespassed onto your property and knocked you down. I owe you a granola bar."

He grinned. "Chocolate chip, please."

From their respective sides of the fence, Abby stretched the crumpled wire while Quinn straightened the bent metal posts. Working together, they reattached a few fence clips, but most had been lost to the dirt. "This should hold for now," she said. "I'll fix it for real later."

"I'll be happy to help. Just let me know when."

"Thanks. I will." All she wanted right now was to stagger inside, doctor her damaged feet, and sort out the swirl of emotions that had been stirred up by her aunt's sexy new neighbor.

———————

Quinn trudged to the pool house, pressing a fist into the knotted muscles surrounding his lower spine. Much as he appreciated the appearance of his surprisingly attractive neighbor (or neighbor's niece…whatever), he could have done without the equine attack that prompted the meeting.

He chuckled at the memory of Abby's barefooted ferocity—ready to do battle in Daffy Duck boxers and a barely there tank top. With her hazel eyes flashing, her cheeks on fire, and a wild cloud of honey-brown hair tumbling over her shoulders, she tempted him to forget how much damn trouble women could be.

In the bathroom, he lowered his boxer-briefs, then twisted around in front of the mirror to assess the damage. Black-and-blue hoofprints marred his lower back. His left butt cheek sported burgundy-and-purple bite marks.

"Admiring your backside?"

At the snide tone of his ex-wife's voice, Quinn snatched up his jeans so quickly his underwear rolled into an uncomfortable wad around his hips. He met her dark eyes in the bathroom mirror. "Melissa, I don't recall inviting you in." And he had never *admired his backside*. Hers, yes. That was what had gotten him into this whole mess—the mess that was his life—in the first place.

He reached back and slammed the bathroom door in her face. She'd rejected him, not the other way around. But that didn't mean she could sashay back into his life whenever she took a notion. "What are you doing here?" he yelled through the closed door.

"I can't have Sean coming here until I know it's safe."

Until she knows it's safe. Right. As if he'd do anything to endanger his own son, who at fifteen was nearly as tall as Quinn and could handle himself in any case. Quinn readjusted his underwear and buttoned his jeans. Following his therapist's advice, he closed his eyes and counted ten cleansing breaths before he wrenched open the bathroom door.

Dressed to impress in a pinstriped girl-suit that impressed him more than he wished it did, Melissa stood with a smirk on her expertly painted face. "You look like hell."

Another deep breath allowed him to walk past his ex-wife

into his small but clean kitchen. With determined civility, he poured water on the fireworks she seemed equally determined to ignite. He knew he had a lot to atone for, so as his therapist suggested, he let her snarky comments slide. They both had to work through their anger and resentment in whatever way worked for them.

For him, it was a determination to keep his mouth shut in the short term. In the long term, he planned to make a fortune he could flap in her face like a red flag.

For her, it was a determination to show him what he was missing in the short term. In the long term, she planned to get along better without him than she had with him.

She had the added secret weapon of snark, but he had to give her that advantage. He'd been absent when she needed him, so she'd learned to take care of herself, then kicked him to the curb when he lost everything. He understood her grievance and was willing to pay the price, but still, it stung. "Would you like a drink?"

Melissa kicked off her red-soled high heels and flung herself onto his new gray couch. "What've you got?"

He opened the refrigerator. "OJ, Coke, and V8."

"I won't be here that long. I just wanted to see where Sean will be staying next weekend, if he decides to come."

If he decides to come. As if the kid would have any choice if his mother even pretended to uphold the court's visitation ruling. Quinn popped the top on a V8 and sucked it down, then tossed the empty can into the trash. He knew better than to engage, but his ability to maintain detachment had its limits. "Feel free to look around."

"Already did that, thanks." She slipped into her shoes and stood. "Can't say I approve of all the prepackaged food in your cupboards, but I guess it won't kill him to eat junk a few days out of the month."

Quinn bit back a scathing comment. Proud he'd managed to keep his fool mouth shut, he followed her out and watched her wobble across the gravel in her high heels, then slide into a shiny, red BMW M6 convertible and drive away.

———

Wolf watched the man walk around the corner of the house and stand by the frog pool, his shoulders slumped, his energy deflated. Wolf hid under the hedge fence that enclosed the farm with its locked gate and all the tasty animal smells. The man glanced in his direction, and Wolf lowered himself to the ground, blending with the leaf clutter beneath the hedge's straggling branches.

The human didn't seem threatening now; not like he had earlier today when he yelled at the panicked donkey who had trespassed. Wolf had watched the commotion from a thicket of brush, ready to defend his new friend Georgia.

But he had made a terrible mistake before by protecting his family when his help wasn't welcome. He hoped his family would return for him, but he didn't deserve it yet. He had to reconcile the two halves of his nature and understand what his human family expected of him, even if it didn't make sense.

He didn't know exactly what he'd done wrong. The whole messy situation had become jumbled in his memory. But even though the details of the incident had blurred in his mind, the ultimate conclusion remained crystal clear.

Out of love, he had made a mistake.

That meant love was dangerous.

Birds flitted among the leaves above his head; a bright-red pair scolded him from the nest they were building. When the man went inside, Wolf would catch one of those birds and fill his shrinking belly. He made that promise to his growling stomach. Then he closed his eyes and brought his energy down low so the man wouldn't sense him lying in wait for a chance to drink, and maybe also to eat.

Every evening, Wolf drank from the green pool and caught

frogs to eat. The bitter taste of frog skin turned his saliva to foam, but the meat and bones and entrails tasted no different from that of a rabbit or rat or mouse. Wolf hardly remembered the taste of the crunchy kibble he had eaten at home.

The wind shifted, a warm breeze blowing along the ground. Wolf lifted his nose and caught the scent of rabbits behind the fence. He had searched for a way in, but failed. He could have snagged a small goat this morning while the fence was down. But the people would have seen him, and humans had strange attitudes about which animals were okay to eat and which were off-limits.

Safety lay in hunting only at night when people hid behind solid walls and dark windows. Light windows meant people might still venture outside. Dark windows meant they would stay inside until morning. Wolf's hungry stomach made it hard to wait for safety, but he knew he must.

By the time the man went inside, the birds had flown into a tall tree. Wolf crawled low along the hedge, ran to the green pool to satisfy his thirst with a few quick laps, then streaked across the road to his hiding place in the cat's-claw forest. In the cool, green shade, he sprawled on his side, closed his eyes, and waited for sleep to silence his hunger. Tonight, when the sun slipped over the horizon, he would hunt.

Chapter 5

THAT EVENING, WITH CHORES DONE, REVA'S TEXT RESPONDED to, and a pound cake baked, Abby assembled her peace offerings in an old wicker basket that she'd found stashed among others above her aunt's kitchen cabinets. A bottle of sparkling cider paired with two cheap wineglasses from Dollar Tree; cheese, olives, and fancy crackers; the pound cake wrapped in a new dish towel and tied with twine; and as promised, a chocolate-chip granola bar.

Part of her hoped he wouldn't be home and she'd be able to leave the basket outside his door. She had included a hand-written note on Bayside Barn stationery that she found in her aunt's rolltop desk:

To Quinn,

Please accept my attempt at a more conventional welcome to the neighborhood than the one you received this morning.

Abby Curtis

P.S. Sorry about my ass biting yours.

The nagging, familiar voice of social anxiety whispered, reminding her of his cryptic comment about *the view* that made her suspect he'd seen more of her skin than he should have.

Instead of letting worry have its way, she went into the laundry room and tossed a scrap of twine into the crate for the new kitten to play with. This time, the kitten didn't flee for cover. Maybe it was beginning to realize that Abby was trying to help. She had doctored the road rash with Betadine and a thin film of Neosporin, and already it was healing up nicely.

In the kitchen, she gave Max the tabby a cat treat. "Please stay off the kitchen counter while I'm gone."

Sure thing, she imagined Max saying, though his slant-eyed smirk told her she shouldn't believe him. So much for all the things Reva had tried to teach her about animal communication. If all males were liars, why bother?

Abby glanced at her reflection in the sliding glass doors. Dressed in a leaf-print dress that brought out the green flecks in her hazel eyes, she looked well enough. But she hoped she hadn't overdone it by curling her hair and wearing mascara and clear lip gloss.

She wasn't interested in Quinn—she knew better by now than to be lured in by a pretty face and a rock-hard body— but she didn't want him to judge her unfavorably either. She didn't want to look like a slob, but she also didn't want to look as if she'd tried too hard. Abby wished she could absorb a little of her aunt's complete disregard for what other people thought of her.

Abby had been that way herself once, but after trusting completely and then losing everything that mattered, she couldn't find her way back. Her recent tendency to worry about everything insisted that she doubt herself.

Georgia barked.

"Okay." Abby picked up the basket and a tiny wisp of courage. "I'm coming."

The setting sun glowed orange over the bay when she and Georgia walked along the hedge and through the iron gates of Bayside Barn. Abby propped one side of the gate open, then she and Georgia crossed the easement to the neighbor's property. The dilapidated house was dark, so they went around back, and Abby tapped on the sliding glass door of the pool house, where the glow of interior lighting indicated a human presence.

Charcoal-gray curtains had been pushed aside. The ceiling fan's globe light revealed brand-new furnishings. A gray couch and rug and overstuffed armchair, a distressed barn-wood coffee table and end tables, a flat-screen TV mounted on the wall across from the couch. No throw pillows, no lamps, no pictures on the walls.

Georgia whined and looked back toward the farm.

"No. We're doing this."

The new neighbor walked into the room shirtless, wearing jeans slung low on his hips and headphones in his ears. The headphones' yellow cord trailed down his toned chest and washboard abs, then twined around his waist and disappeared into his back pocket.

"Lord above, Georgia. Would you look at that?"

Unimpressed, Georgia whined and pawed Abby's leg.

"No, I said. No."

Realizing that he must not have heard the knock, Abby waved. But he kept going to the small kitchen and opened the fridge. She tapped on the glass door again. He took out a beer and turned, then saw her. His eyes opened wide. He set the beer aside, pulled out his headphones, and opened the sliding glass door. "Hey. Is there a goat in my pool or something?"

Georgia ran inside and leaped onto a chair.

"Georgia, no." Abby felt a blush spread up her neck and into her cheeks. "You weren't invited."

"It's fine." He stepped away from the door. "Come on in."

Abby handed over the basket. "This is a housewarming/apology basket." She couldn't help but notice the hoof-shaped bruises on his lower back. "I'm sorry Elijah hurt you. I'm sure he didn't mean to, but he can't resist sweet-tasting treats." Out of breath with anxiety, she powered through her prepared greeting. "I hope we can pretend this morning never happened and start over again."

He set the basket on the coffee table and held out a hand. "Quinn Lockhart."

She put her hand in his. "Abby Curtis, house-sitting for my aunt Reva. Welcome to the neighborhood."

"Thank you, Abby." His fingers wrapped around hers, his grip strong but gentle, his palm callused but warm. Up close, blue eyes the color of new denim smiled into hers. His touch and his smile melted the crusty outer layer of her anxiety.

He let go of her hand. "Have a seat while I put on a shirt."

Abby perched on the couch, crossed her legs, then uncrossed them. She inhaled and blew out a deep breath to release another layer of anxiety. The room smelled of fresh paint, newly dyed fabric, and recently milled wood.

Georgia's restless gaze tracked something outside the glass door. She whined, a worried furrow between her brows.

Abby leaned forward. "You see something out there?"

Quinn came into the room wearing a plain white T-shirt that wasn't too tight but still somehow clung to every muscle. He sat beside her on the couch and slid the basket closer. "Hmm." He held up the bottle of cider. "This looks interesting."

Abby was more of a wine girl herself, but after twisting and turning over the decision of what to bring, she'd settled on cider, in case the new neighbor didn't drink anything containing alcohol. "I hope you like it."

He set the two glasses on the coffee table and opened the bottle. "Anything I share with you will be better than a lonely beer by myself."

Smooth talker. The sort she'd already fallen for once too often. "Please don't feel obligated to share. I meant it as a gift, not an intrusion." Her nervousness lifted her like an overfilled helium balloon. She half stood, then sat again.

Since she'd moved in with her aunt this spring, she had learned to handle hundreds of school kids along with their adult teachers and chaperones. But social situations requiring small talk still made her palms sweat. "I only came to welcome you to the neighborhood and apologize for Elijah's rude behavior this morning. I'm very sorry about the whole thing."

He poured cider into the two glasses and handed one to her. "Apology accepted, incident forgotten, starting over. Remember?"

About the Author

Carolyn Brown is a *New York Times*, *USA Today*, *Wall Street Journal*, *Publishers Weekly*, and #1 Amazon and #1 *Washington Post* bestselling author, as well as a RITA finalist. She is the author of more than one hundred novels and several novellas. She's a recipient of the Bookseller's Best Award and the prestigious Montlake Diamond Award, as well as a three-time recipient of the National Reader's Choice Award. Brown has been published for more than twenty years, and her books have been translated into nineteen foreign languages.

She's been married for more than fifty years to Mr. B, and they have three smart, wonderful, amazing children, fifteen grandchildren, and too many great-grands to keep track of. When she's not writing, she likes to plot new stories in her backyard with her tomcat, Boots Randolph Terminator

Outlaw, who protects the yard from all kinds of wicked varmints like crickets, locusts, and spiders.

Carolyn can be found online at carolynlbrown.com, facebook.com/carolynbrownbooks, on Instagram @carolyn brownbooks, and on Twitter @thecarolynbrown.

Also by Carolyn Brown

WELCOME BACK TO RAMBLING, TEXAS

From acclaimed author June Faver: the women of Rambling tackle small-town living in the heart of Texas Hill Country

Reggie Lee Stafford is a hometown girl living in Rambling, the small Texas town where she was born. As a single mother, her world revolves around her young daughter and her beloved job at the local newspaper. But her peaceful life is turned upside down when Frank Bell—the bane of Reggie's teenage existence—returns to town to claim his vast inheritance.

"June Faver is a must-read author."

—*Harlequin Junkie*

For more info about Sourcebooks's books and authors, visit:

sourcebooks.com

THAT DEEP RIVER FEELING

Romance has an Alaska homecoming in this
bold, sexy series from Jackie Ashenden

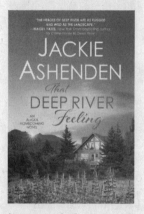

Zeke Calhoun doesn't care much about Deep River, but he'll do just
about anything to keep the last promise he made—to look out for
his best friend's sister.

As the sole police officer in Deep River, Morgan West won't be
bossed around, but Zeke is irresistible. He's tough, challenging, and
all kinds of sexy, but getting involved is the last thing on Morgan's
mind...

**"The heroes of Deep River are as rugged
and wild as the landscape."**

—Maisey Yates, *New York Times* bestselling author

For more info about Sourcebooks's books and authors, visit:

sourcebooks.com

HOPE ON THE RANGE

Welcome to the Turn Around Ranch:
charming contemporary cowboy romance from
USA Today bestselling author Cindi Madsen

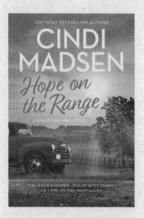

Brady Dawson has been in love with Tanya Greer for as long as he
can remember. But running the Turn Around Ranch with his family
doesn't leave much downtime for relationships. Now that Tanya is
contemplating a move to the city, it looks like he might never get
his chance... Faced with the realization that he might lose Tanya
forever, he'll have to cowboy up and prove to Tanya that the Turn
Around Ranch is the perfect place to call home.

"Feel-good romance...full of witty charm."

—A. J. Pine, *USA Today* bestselling author

For more info about Sourcebooks's books and authors, visit:

sourcebooks.com